BROOD X

BROOD X

JOSHUA DYSART

Illustrated by M.K. Perker

Brood X by Joshua Dysart

Illustrations by M.K. Perker
Cover design by Julie Metz Design
Interior design by Amy Sumerton

All inquiries should be addressed to:
    TKO Studios, LLC
    1325 Franklin Avenue
    Suite 545
    Garden City, NY 11530

TKO STUDIOS is a registered trademark

Visit our website at tkopresents.com

First Edition
ISBN: 978-1-952203-28-2

Printed in the United States of America

_For Ann Nickerson, who taught me
how to read; Jeronimo Quinones,
who showed me what to read;
Mom, for letting me read anything
I wanted; and Kelly Bruce,
who reads it all first._

—Joshua

For my daughter, Leyla.

—M.K.

There are fifteen broods of cicadas that emerge in thirteen- to seventeen-year cycles throughout the eastern United States. In 1953, the largest North American emergence in recorded history occurred. Some parts of the country reported over a million cicadas per square mile. As many as 40,000 cicada nymphs burrowed out from under a single oak tree in only a few hours. The emergence belonged to the cicada progeny with the farthest range and greatest concentration.

It is known as Brood X.

I

Summer. 1953.

THE THIRTEEN-TON TRUCK has long since rattled off the paved tar of State Road 60. Now its diesel roar presses deep into the Indiana wilderness, pitching and yawing as it gears up and down the long, unused logging road that winds through the wooded hills.

There are seven men sitting in the uncovered bed any way they can, their bones banging about. They've cooked in the sun all the way up from Louisville, their grime-smeared caps or flat brim hats rimmed with sweat. But now the logging road has finally plunged them into tree cover, and the canopy's shadow, dappled with winking light, is a respite as they roll mile after mile into the isolated woods.

The seven squinting, drawn faces jostle and sway with the truck's labors. The men are all crackers, pink and splotchy, or red like boiled lobster, or leathered brown from years of back-bending in the sun. Except for a single Negro, named Victor, with big hands. Victor looks like he's had his nose broken and poorly set once or twice in his life.

Quent sits in the rear of the bed, his back against the cab. He's the least showered among them, and his work clothes are the most worn. Quent's been drifting for a while. He slept in the alleyway behind a warehouse near the pickup point last night.

Quent watches a man named James, with beet-flushed cheeks and a disturbance of red hair spilling out from beneath an army service cap, take a tug on a flask he's been periodically visiting for the better part of the day. James has enough sense to wordlessly pass the flask around to the others now and then, and he sends it back out now. Some drink from it, some don't.

"Long ride for just a couple weeks' work," a clenched-jawed man in his early thirties with two first names, David Bruce, says loudly enough to be heard over the rattling of the truck. He takes James's flask and passes it on, not sipping from it. "You all from Kentucky or . . . ?" The other men shake their heads or let out with a "naw." It's too loud and uncomfortable for conversation. "You mean we left out of Louisville, and not one of you boys is Kentucky bred? Geezus help me, I'm with a bunch of knockabouts."

The flask eventually comes around to Quent and he takes it, maybe too eagerly. He's the only one of the men to draw on it twice. Immediately feeling a little lighter, it strikes Quent that they're a pretty desperate sight, this crew.

There's an old geezer with thin lips whose face rests in a joyless smile, seeming too on in years for the kind of labor they're setting out to do. There are two very young-looking men, maybe in their mid-twenties. An almost boyish one with sallow eyes in dark, deep-set sockets, and a Jewy-looking kid with strong, dense shoulders and a greaser duck-ass haircut, his dark curls oiled tight and flat. Something about the age range of the group seems unusual, and there's a general air to each of the workers that Quent recognizes in different ways but can't quite put into words.

The ragged logging road is endless. Deeper and deeper into the dense Indiana woods it takes them. As red-headed James caps his returned flask and slides it into his pocket, he yells over the din of the truck, "Guess this ain't the kinda job where we all go to the local for a beer after a day's work, eh?"

The truck rolls into the wide construction site clearing. Canopy shade gives way again to the midday wash of sunlight. The men squint against it.

Ian, the truck driver, petite and dressed properly in an out-of-style, tweed flat cap and snug weskit vest, brings the vehicle to a stop and tugs the pull-button so that the engine rumbles down into a sigh. The only sounds the big machine makes now are cooling ticks and a tinny voice from the radio still playing in the cab. Communist secret agents, Julius and Ethel Rosenberg, will be put to death in a couple of weeks. Senator McCarthy, whose voice is familiar to every American, calls out for any man seen as a danger to the welfare of this great country to be investigated. Ian kills the radio. After hours of the truck's growl, the comparative silence seems supernatural.

Standing, stretching, some more limber than others, the men drop from the back of the truck. Victor offers to help the old man down, but the geezer doesn't take his hand. He ends up laboring to climb down on his own until the strong kid with the greaser haircut, flashing an easy smile, steps up to help him. The old man takes the white hand.

Ian comes around, so short that he has to look up to meet the faces of the others, and they all stand there, surveying where they'll be spending the next several weeks. It's a large glade. Work has already been done to deforest it. Heavy construction equipment and earth movers are here, driven in and dropped off by flatbeds at some point, which might explain why the logging road is in such rough shape. There's a big dozer and a power crawler shovel that rides high on mud-caked treads. There's a backhoe; a squat wheel loader; several Caterpillar diesel generators scattered around on small hitch trailers; a heavy, reversible drum concrete mixer that stands about ten feet tall at the charge chute, with a trailer-mounted concrete pump parked next to it; and a gyratory rock crusher that looks like a combat turret on wheels.

Wooden boxes, likely filled with diaphragm pumps, gas hammers, and other tools (since the men were told not to bring their own), are stacked near bags of cement mixer, sand, and gravel. Long, tall piles of steel rebar rods are lashed and heaped into several small hills alongside a stack of pick-axes and shovels. The trees that once filled this space are also stacked and stripped, repurposed as lumber for the project. Several table-saw stations surround the lumber stores like posted guards. Three big diesel fuel tanks on trailers tower at the back of the site next to a large water tank with several forty-gallon drums arranged around their base. There are piles of ducts, plumbing and electrical equipment, and a small assortment of heavy steel doors waiting to be fitted to some future structure. The doors lay flat against the earth so that it seems as if a man could open them and descend into a myth-ological underground to face the darkest aspects of himself.

There's a large Temper tent for the men's shared quarters and, pushed off to one side of the clearing, a covered outdoor kitchen and eating area. Parked alongside the kitchen is a rounded, blue-and-white travel trailer shaped like a funny dot on wheels, large enough for two people, and a '51 Chevy pickup, which probably brought the trailer in. Latrines and showers grace the opposite side of the construction site from the kitchen, near the wood and supply piles.

The men are first greeted by Mac, who barked alongside the big truck as it pulled into the clearing. Lean and athletic with ears like a bat, Mac now presses his muzzle into offering hands and sniffs at pant legs. Big man Victor kneels and takes a tongue to the face. "Looks like a kelpie mix! We had some back in Alabama when I was a boy. You gotta work these mothers or they'll drive you crazy," he says happily.

"Hello the crew!" A man and woman approach. Hard faced, older, German stock, blue eyes set in dirty faces. "I'm Samuel Stern, project manager and the concrete finisher. This here's my wife, Fanny. She'll be our camp cook and caretaker while we're out here." Fanny nods, shielding her fair eyes from the sun to get a read on the men's faces. Freckles splash the bridge of her nose.

Ian is the first to reach out and shake Samuel's hand. Samuel nods to the truck Ian has just parked, "This here your rig, son?"

"No, sir. I picked it up in Louisville. Thought it might belong to you. You're not the one who hired us?"

"No. I ain't never met the boss man. Think he's up north somewhere. But we've gotten checks. They spend good. We were able to pay the crew who cleared this site, so the work's honest. Let me show you fellas the construction area before we get settled in."

Mac bounces ahead as the men move to the large, staked-out, stringed-off, empty square at the heart of the clearing. Fanny turns back toward the shade of the dining area without a word.

"Here's the footprint of the bomb shelter," Samuel says.

"Big son-of-a-bitch," clenched-jawed David Bruce says.

"We'll go over the plans during supper. You'll all find you'll be doing a little bit of everything out here, then taking the lead on your specialties. We're basically building a better underground bunker than any house I ever lived in. I think we've got a rich end-of-the-worlder on our hands, boys."

David Bruce shakes his head. "Tell you what though, these goddamned communists are turning the whole world to shit. We shoulda pushed on to Moscow when we had the chance."

Red-headed James laughs, says nothing, pulls on the brim of his army service cap, and hits his flask.

Samuel sees this. "What's your job here, son?"

"Metal worker, Mr. Stern."

"Okay, well, we start digging first thing in the morning and there's not a one of you who won't be helping us make that hole, so let's get some rest tonight," Samuel says.

Tin plates, mostly empty, orbit the blueprints of the bomb shelter laying atop the long picnic table in the eating and kitchen area. Supper started before dusk, but now it's nightfall and the men are still sitting. The climate is accommodating, and moths bomb the naked light bulbs clipped to the wooden beams of the kitchen tent. Somewhere a generator grumbles.

The men drag on cigarettes and drink whiskey coffee. Some hold their empty plates down for Mac to clean. Fanny, having delivered dinner, has faded away, retiring to the trailer.

The strong kid with the greaser haircut shines his easy smile toward Victor. "Sir, I've been meaning to say, but I've been a little bashful, I recognized you soon as I saw you. You used to box in Cincinnati, ain't I right?"

Victor doesn't say anything, but a grin spreads across his face and his eyes suddenly catch the light. The other men all turn their attention to the conversation.

The kid keeps at it. "Sure I'm right! My old man used to haul me out to the bouts. You're a southpaw. Heavyweight. I remember!"

Victor cracks. "Yeah . . . yeah, that's me."

Haircut leans across the table and shakes Victor's hand enthusiastically. "I knew it! Man, you were a powerhouse. Fast as hell too. Victor 'Jab' Jenkins! Yes, sir. I'm Hank. It's real good to meet you, Mr. Jenkins."

David Bruce cuts in. "What's your job here, Hank?"

"Heavy equipment operator, sir."

"Equipment operator? And this one over here's a journey-man electrician?" David Bruce points an accusatory finger at the sallow-eyed young man who had introduced himself as Baxter back when the day was still young. Now Baxter smiles nervously, ill at ease from the attention turned on him. "Where'd you children get that kind of experience?" David Bruce asks. Maybe he means to be playful, but the way he tightens his jaw whenever he's not gabbing just makes him seem mean.

Haircut Hank affords David Bruce a brief, jovial glance to register that he's in on the man's ribbing and then turns his attention back to Victor. "I used to hit the bag too, now and then. Nothing like you, though. Why'd you stop?"

Victor shakes his head, pushing away some small, encroaching sadness. "Ahh, I just got too tired of the monkey business."

Hank nods and says knowingly to the rest of the table, "He means the mob."

Victor doesn't counter, but he doesn't stop smiling about being recognized either.

The conversation is sparse. Mostly the men talk about what they're here to do and how they plan on doing it: Victor is the lead carpenter; old man Homer the engineer; David Bruce is dealing with the plumbing; and petite Ian, in his funny vest and flat cap, is the mechanic. When they turn to Quent, quiet and alone at the end of the long table, and inquire about his experience, he grins uncomfortably.

"Oh, I'm just here to work," he says, not looking anyone in the eye. They all know what that means. Quent wasn't hired for any special skills, he made the crew simply because he was willing. The men have met a thousand Quents in their time on other jobs. Labor grunts, bottom of the ladder, existing simply as another pair of hands, and there solely to do what he's told. No one asks him any more questions, and a pause settles over the conversation.

Old man Homer crinkles his eyes as smoke from his hand-rolled cigarette curls into his face, but he doesn't move the hand that holds it away. "Almost time for the cicadas to come up, you know? The ones that only come every few some odd years."

"You mean locusts?" Victor asks, but the old man acts like Victor isn't there. Victor, like sallow-eyed Baxter, hasn't been saying much. It felt good to be singled out by Hank, but Victor understands that he's got to take the temperature of the others when he's surrounded by white men. Between this and Homer refusing his help getting down from the truck earlier, Victor knows how Homer feels about him being here.

"I was a boy last time a big one of those came around," muses Quent, maybe trying to save face with the men, be less awkward. "It was something, all right."

Homer finds his voice for Quent. "Seen it a few times now. Real special, but I'm not sure that doing work, especially down in the ground, makes a whole lot of sense. I'm probably wrong though. Probably don't make no difference."

"Yeah. You're pretty old," Victor says, driving on with Homer now. "Seen a lot. You sure you should be out here doing this kinda work?" And everyone looks at Victor like he isn't one of them, even though they all thought that same thing about Homer the minute they met him.

Homer doesn't even look over at the Black man, he just stares ahead, but it also seems like he knows Victor is telling some version of the truth. "I'm just an engineer, here to make sure you all don't fuck it up."

"Doesn't seem like that's how the division of labor is going to go down, old man," Victor pushes.

Homer looks at Victor with soft, gray eyes. "I hit on hard times when my wife died. I been on the hunt for work wherever I can get it. I'm just trying to eat like the rest of you. I won't slow no one down." He pushes himself up from the table with all the difficulties of a body that's labored too long, no matter how hard he tries not to show it.

Victor glances around the table at the other men, his friendly smile gone. He's let Homer's attitude toward him activate a part of his personality he's not proud of, but here, with the flush of subtle anger still warming his face, he's not quite ready to stand down. So he gathers the men up in his pugilist gaze. Only the mechanic, Ian, and project manager, Samuel, meet his eyes. The others find plenty to silently interest them. It goes unspoken that every man there, including Victor, knows what Homer's talking about. They all got word of this job last minute. They all feel lucky to be here for one reason or another.

After dinner they unload the truck and carry their packs to the shared sleeping tent. Red-headed James says it reminds him of Army basic with its two rows of cots and large, screened windows. It's Quent's instinct to lash out at James with sarcastic venom—*Yeah, we see the Army cap. We get it, you're a fucking war hero*—but Quent keeps his peace and moves to claim a cot. It's the first time he won't be sleeping on the ground in weeks.

Sitting, David Bruce unpacks a .45 and a bible, and everybody sees him place them both in the padlocked trunk at the foot of his cot. When Baxter, whose cot is next to David's, nods toward the handgun David Bruce smiles at him. "What's a gun between men in the middle of nowhere, eh?" Baxter turns his back to David Bruce without a word and lies down on his bunk. David Bruce grins at the others, but it's late, and tomorrow promises to be a long day. No one entertains the exchange.

Once the lights are turned out and the generator killed, the whole world goes black as the inside of a cave. At some point, Ian, still awake, hears Quent whisper something in his sleep, whimper, then fall silent. Much later the faint foraging of an unseen creature, maybe Mac, maybe a permanent resident of these woods, is heard outside the tent as it rustles, distantly, through the dreams of the men.

First light finds Ian already awake, far from the camp clearing, sitting on a rock surrounded by woods. He's been here for maybe an hour, since before the sky started to turn. He stares at nothing but the changing glow. His mind is empty, ready to be filled by the coming day's thoughts and experiences. A flow of deer enters his field of vision. Cautiously, they feed from bruise-colored foliage. How beautiful, Ian thinks. How fragile and strange everything is.

The men begin breaking the earth after an early breakfast. They wrench it up in boulder-sized clumps with the great, smoke-belching machines. Duck-ass cut Hank and red-headed James control the machines like riders on dinosaurs, while the others lean into shovels and pickaxes, wearing heavy working gloves to protect their hands. James has a little knowledge of operating the machinery, but David Bruce can't let go of how young Hank is to be an operator. He leans on his pickaxe, shirt soaked with sweat, and opines, "Those people control all the banks that pay for construction up in New York, where he's probably from. Least they can do is teach their spoiled-shit kids how to do a little real work, I guess."

Hank isn't there to hear this, he's lost in the roar of the backhoe cab, but Quent is, and he challenges David Bruce's logic. "Now what the hell would a rich Jew be doing out here with us humping earth in the middle of fuck-all Indiana?" He doesn't even bring up that Hank doesn't have an upper East Coast accent.

The world gets hot. The work is hard. The dust rises. The men try to wet the earth as best they can, but their water tank holds the same water they'll be drinking so they're judicious with it. Many tie shirts around their faces, and the dirt that would've been inhaled collects in the fabric around their covered mouths and noses. It sands into their eyes and grooves into their tear ducts. The men turn the color of the earth. It's like this for days. And as they make a great hole in the ground, they dig into one another as well. Quiet, sallow-eyed Baxter, comes off as squirrelly, and David Bruce likes to point this out to the others. Most of them don't seem comfortable around Victor at all. They fuck with him in small ways that make him long for home. None of them feels completely comfortable amongst each other, but that's not the kind of thing they can voice.

On and on, deeper and deeper, dig the men.

By the time the cicada nymphs emerge, the men have spent close to two weeks working on the shelter.

They've dug a thirty-foot deep, three-thousand-square-foot hole and laid substantial rebar reinforced footing to take the extra weight of future walls and beams. Victor has built base forms from plywood. They all spent a single, hectic, choreographed, labor-intensive morning doing a monolithic concrete pour for the footing, foundation, and descending entry steps, putting all personal frictions aside to work as a team during the oozing rush. They've constructed pads and chases where the electricity, climate control, air pumps, and plumbing will go; built and placed even more wooden forms for the outer walls, leaving a backfill ditch that circles the perimeter of the structure like a moat; and installed several sump pumps.

The huge mound of displaced soil from the construction hole has been swarming with tiny, confused, alien nymphs torn from the ground before the conditions were right. But now, on a perfect June evening, the whole of the earth suddenly belches forth a surge of crawling brown bugs as far as the men can see.

They boil out from under the roots of trees. They fall in waves into the construction hole, dense and helpless and scrambling across the newly poured concrete foundation at the bottom of the shelter. The nymphs cover the fallen trees the workers are planning to set the roof form of the shelter with, and the men race to shine powerful lights on the lumber stacks as night falls. They sweep the lumber clean of the nymphs and tie the stacks tightly with burlap to keep the coming adults from laying their eggs in the wood.

The nymphs climb. The trunks of the trees look to be breathing. The nymphs seek higher ground across the entirety of Indiana. Far beyond the vision and comprehension of the men, they climb. They climb in parts of eastern Illinois and across half of Pennsylvania. They climb in swaths of the Virginias and Tennessee. They climb from long rags of land across states as far down as Georgia. They climb by the millions. The heavy machinery, the tents, the trucks, these are all free of them, but the natural world undulates with the movement of the nymphs. A countless ancestral horde, each aching to grow, to propagate, to complete an ancient transformation. It is a dark marvel to the men.

The nymphs undergo their final molting that evening. Their prepubescent bodies harden, become constricting, limiting. They heave with their backs, struggling to crack the shells of their former selves. They emerge, adults, white as bone, then darken rapidly. Their eyes shift to a red as vibrant as newly spilt blood.

The work on the bomb shelter continues uneventfully for the next week. The foundation is long cured, and the work of wall building with concrete, core-filled bricks begins.

Above, in the trees, the new cicada bodies have been hardening, maturing. Their thoraxes have turned black. Their wings, translucent, are now shot through with orange veins. With tremendous biological imperative, the males, collectively ready, begin to sing.

* * *

The men stopped having much to say to one another at dinner after a few days into the work. Now they clack dominoes and play Omaha hold 'em with a deck of cards. Hank shows the others how to pull off a three-card monte while flashing his easy smile.

David Bruce says, "Of course that boy knows how to hustle." But he says it lightly so he can get away with it as a joke, then clenches his jaw.

Hank knows what he means. Rarely does Hank's smile drop, but it does so now. He throws the cards down and asks David Bruce, "Which is it? Do we run the world banks or are we two-bit hustlers?"

David Bruce just smiles and turns away because he knows that if he says, "What's the difference?" it'll just cause more trouble.

A portable radio squawks from the corner of the eating area. It's hooked to a makeshift antenna made from a metal cooking strainer set atop the roof. Sometimes sallow-eyed Baxter and faded Quent can get them to pipe in honky-tonk, but David Bruce and Ian the mechanic usually want to hear the news. Tonight they learn that the Rosenbergs have been executed.

"I wish I coulda seen them do their last jig in that chair," says project manager Samuel Stern. Fanny, gathering dishes, gives her husband a disapproving look.

David Bruce can't leave it alone. "They ought to investigate every Jew in America, like the senator says. Let's see whose side they're really on. What's the harm in it?"

Hank smirks at David Bruce as if he's ridiculous, but Hank also clenches his fist tight so that the knuckles turn white. He lets David Bruce see this. David Bruce gets the message and moves to another part of the dining area.

Now a man who claims to be an FBI agent growls from

out of the little radio speaker. "For nine years I was living on the brink of a volcano, a volcano called Communism, a volcano which is centered in Soviet Russia but which is erupting right here in America and all over the world . . ."

It's then that the cicada song comes to the attention of the men. At first an unconscious hum down in the basement of the men's minds, it rises, eventually drowning out the radio, impossible to ignore.

The male cicadas have gathered into huge clusters out in the darkening woods. They are calling in chorus to the females. *It's time*, they say. *This is our time. Weeeeewhoaaaaaaaaa*, they say. Their song, loud and constant and resonating, even over the sound of the generator, reveals new dimensions.

Suddenly cicadas are in the eating area. Flying. Crowding the naked light bulbs. Females, hungry for the song, clicking their wings, bang against the men's faces and land in their food. The men leap to their feet, cursing and swatting at the bug-desire all around them.

Later, inside the enclosed sleeping tent, the men lay awake on their bunks, not speaking, because who can hear anything other than the song? It rattles through their bodies and vibrates in their brains. They each begin to find something different in it. Some hear human voices, some hear engines like the ones in the big digging machines, some hear the whitewater babble of rivers they grew up near. Only red-headed James manages any real sleep, and that's just because he's more loaded tonight than usual.

The men wake to see the entire world outside their living quarters sheathed in cicadas. The surface of trees, their equipment, and the earth itself roils in the daylight. Where the landscape is free of the swell of bugs, exposed and visible, it's like the drifting spots on the surface of the sun, flowing and shifting in shape, contracting and expanding.

"I don't remember it ever being like this," Homer says.

Quent nods in agreement, though he's only seen one big emergence in his life.

Mac walks around scooping them into his narrow mouth, gorging, crunching for hours, cicada innards coloring his now-thick saliva. He smacks and smacks until he vomits great heaps of bile and masticated bugs onto more living, crawling bugs, and then he eats the vomit drenched bugs and begins again. Like it's a job. Like it's a war.

The men spend the day trying to establish a temporary roof on the bomb shelter before they can begin work on a permanent one. They lay the wood materials, but no one is certain that the lumber hasn't been compromised by cicada eggs, or what that would even mean. They'll be pouring concrete once they build a rebar reinforced frame, and they need the lumber form to do its part and stand the weight. Work is especially hard now. The men spend as much time standing around wondering at the novel order of things as they do working. The cicada song never stops.

They manage to close off the eating area with tarps, and Fanny spends the better part of an afternoon trying to clean it of bugs. During dinner they blare the radio as loud as they can in the hope of being able to hear it over the cicadas' mating call. Homer says he's never heard the summer cicadas sing at night like this. Teresa Brewer sings "Till I Waltz with You Again" over the little radio, but it's turned so loud that it's just static now, bringing even more buzzing chaos into the world than before. Conversation, never a rich well, has completely dried up. The men have only their cards and dominoes.

They all drink after-dinner coffee, their bodies slumped against the weight of the song outside. When they stack their tin plates for Fanny to wash, Quent sees Mac finishing Homer's coffee. The old man has absently set his metal mug down on the bench next to him, low enough for Mac to snake his tongue into. Quent figures Mac is in rough shape from eating all those damn bugs. Probably thirsty as hell and probably trying to settle his stomach. Homer seems to move slower after dinner, his eyes narrowed more than usual. Hank, whose duck-cut is beginning to grow out and lose its precision, asks the old man if he's all right, but Homer waves him off.

When they wake the next day from whatever sleep they've managed to get, they find Homer dead in his bunk, foamed at the mouth and smelling of his own shit.

"MUST'VE BEEN a heart attack," Samuel Stern says, standing with the others around Homer's cot, looking down on his lifeless form. Homer's foamy mouth is locked in a frozen gasp, horrified at his own death.

"Doesn't look like one to me," Fanny says.

"Now what do you know about it?" Samuel asks his wife. Fanny traces the Christian cross on herself, forehead to chest, shoulder to shoulder, and heads off into the cicada landscape to find Mac and feed him some breakfast other than bugs.

Sallow-eyed Baxter, who rarely talks, says softly, "We gotta get him to the nearest town, whatever that is."

"It's Sellersburg. But it's not nowhere near to close by," Ian the mechanic says.

"Maybe the hospital there might be able to hold him until our employer can deal with getting him shipped back to wherever he came from," Baxter says.

"I don't even know if there is a hospital in Sellersburg." Ian sighs. He looks around at the men gathered about the cot like it's already Homer's funeral and they're sinking him into the ground right here and now.

David Bruce speaks up, wiping the day's first sweat from

his brow. "Let me make a proposal, and don't give me shit for this. But I say we put him on ice and finish the work here. We could've used Homer for the roof pour, but I think most of us have been doing this long enough that we can do it on our own. We already got the form up. We can manage the rest of this without an engineer. Let's get it done and get paid sooner rather than later. There's a large enough cooler, we just have to keep a generator running at night. And hell, we might not even have to do that if we cool it through the day and keep it in the shade." The other men are silent, so David Bruce continues, "What's going to happen out here once we run him in? They gonna shut down construction? A heart attack's not a big deal for a man Homer's age, but like this weird fucker Baxter says, where does he even come from? Who's going to take care of it? Samuel, you going to write a check from our employer's checkbook for some crazy ass miscellaneous thing like this before you get a chance to talk to him about it?"

A wail of sorrow from Fanny off in the unseen distance breaks the conversation so that none of the men have to agree before they run out to find what's got her so upset. Samuel leads the pack, remembering that the last thing he did was snap at his wife. He calls after her with worried care in his voice.

Mac had crawled up under the power shovel to die in the night. Fanny is kneeling to peer in at him, her hands over her mouth, her simple cotton dress speckled with cicadas caught in its fabric. Samuel groans as soon as he sees his lifeless dog. Everyone generally seems more moved by the death of Mac than by old man Homer lying dead on his cot back in the tent.

Hank wonders aloud, "You think it had something to do with all those cicadas he's been eating?"

Baxter, more talkative in the face of tragedy, is skeptical.

"Aren't these things just protein and eyes and stuff? I don't think that'd kill him."

Quent shakes his head, furrows his brow and draws his mouth tightly like he has something to say, but it never comes.

They take breakfast late, and Fanny's efforts are even more uninspired than usual.

Ian brings back David Bruce's idea as they eat. "You know, I have to concur. We're so close to finishing the shelter. We could just push on through and get out of this place. That old man dying out here is as natural as anything else."

David Bruce slaps his hand down on the long dining table, happy to have an ally, but startling gentle Ian. "More natural than those fucking bugs! Yes! That's what I'm saying. Homer don't give a shit. We'll take him back to civilization with us when we're done." No one disagrees.

They clean out one of the two big freezers, wrap Homer in the blankets from his cot without washing his body and close the lid on him.

Samuel is seen holding his wife through the cica-da-blotted, open screen window of the Sterns' trailer. They rock each other through the loss of their dog. When Samuel goes to bury Mac, Baxter and Quent offer to help. No one else does. It's deep into the morning before the men start work on the bomb shelter.

Later that day, as the sky fades orange into evening, a violent swoop of starlings blows into the camp.

The collective body of the murmuration is close to the ground. The sun is low but still the shadow shapes of the birds pitch and roll over the men like racing storm clouds. The men run for cover. The starlings are taking advantage of the cleared area to frenzy-feed on cicadas. Hundreds of snapping, pecking, charging beaks screech and clap. Thousands of wings whip and flex, like a single great swath of black fabric lashing in a gale.

Most of the men make it clear of the birds, but James gets caught trying to run for the dining tent. Panicked and humbled by the inky swoop, he kneels and covers his head so that the birds pass over and around him. They are a marauding horde, a squall long past hungry, still consuming in mindless celebration of endless bounty. When the starlings are gone as suddenly as they came, James's face and hands have been cut, his red hair has gone weedy and wild, and there's no noticeable dent in the cicada population.

"Motherfuck!" James yells out, at first crawling his way to the dining tent on his hands and knees, then catching some idea of the sight he must be and cautiously standing. He is searching the sky, now empty of starlings, as if they were never even there, like they were his demons alone. "Motherfuck!" he yells again, looking from face to face as the men stare out at him from inside the dining tent, astonished. It's one of those sunsets where one can see both the moon and the sun in the same heaven, and ponder more clearly the celestial relationships of great and powerful things.

James drinks more than usual at dinner.

Ian the mechanic asks, "How'd you manage to carry so much whiskey out here in your one pack, James?"

Ian's question seems earnest, but Victor jokes, "Boy ain't got no clothes, just carrying seventy-five pounds a sauce." Victor likes to call a honky "boy," using the privilege of his physical stature to get away with it. It is the only privilege any of them afford him.

Hank laughs. Samuel laughs. James doesn't laugh. He glares at Victor with bloodshot eyes.

Later that night, wet-lipped and staring at his food, James says something about northern France back in '44 and how he dragged a man with no legs through the mud, and now he's not afraid of shit. But he's slurring his words so fiercely that it sounds like he's speaking a different language to the other men.

* * *

Some of every workday is spent shoveling cicadas out of the bunker and out from under the treads of the machinery. Ian finds them gumming up the gears of the large cement mixer drum and spends much of his time working to keep it in order.

The men work late one evening preparing the concrete mix to pour into the wooden forms for the thick and sturdy beams of the structure. Hank and David Bruce get into a rough tussle of words after David Bruce calls Jews commies again. Hank seems to have lost his patience for it, and David Bruce backs down, again, when Hank starts working his fists open and closed like he's pumping himself up to swing.

Maybe it's just because they're working past dinner time, but the high decibel buzzing made up of a million little ticking bugs seems louder than usual.

While David and Hank throw words, Baxter wanders from the unfinished work in a stumbling daze, needing to be free of the rising potential for violence. The other men call to him, but he doesn't seem to hear them. He walks off to the edge of the clearing and is soon found by Quent. Baxter is staring off into the black night, holding himself gently like Quent has seen women do.

"Those bugs sound like the ocean to me," Baxter tells him. "Like how waves are always shifting and making sounds. Looks like the ocean too, at night, out here. Like how when you look out and the darkness just goes on and on, forever, like a kind of infinity. You know?"

"I've never seen the ocean in person," Quent says. Quent had been thinking about telling Baxter that maybe he should talk more. That his kind of quiet watching makes stupid people nervous, and he's just making it harder on himself with the others. But now that he's heard Baxter actually lean into a conversation, Quent thinks it's probably best if Baxter keeps his peace in general, so he just walks away, leaving Baxter alone. The other men have begun to ostracize the boy, and Quent wants to keep his head down and not get too affiliated, as if whoever Baxter is as a person is somehow contagious.

The next day, while setting up to pour the beams of the shelter, red-headed James, tasked with helping Ian keep bugs clear from the gears of the large mixer, falls through the wide-open loading hopper and into the massive, rolling drum filled with churning concrete.

When the accident occurs, none of the men are nearby, and all are in eyeshot of one another except for Ian and Victor. Ian is the first to yell for help. He's barely heard over the machinery and the insect song.

Inside the drum James is pulled under by the thick sludge, and then crumbled and twisted by the interior rotating blades of the mixer until swirls of red, in great circular patterns, begin to form in the battleship gray surface of the mix.

The men, running, convene at the mixer, where Ian and Victor have already arrived. They get the tumbler powered down and Samuel Stern races up the ladder to the inexplicably uncovered mouth of the drum some ten feet off the ground. Whatever is left of James is jammed down in the bottom of the belly of the thing, under a thousand gallons of morass sludge. The horrifying nature of it all causes Samuel to almost lose his footing on the ladder.

"I didn't see what happened," Ian the mechanic says, greatly distraught. "I-I was on the other side of the machine. I heard a scream, and then he just wasn't up there anymore." Ian turns to Victor. "Where were you? Did you see it?"

Victor shakes his head vigorously, the men's gaze on him. "I was just coming back from the shitter, man. I didn't see anything."

"He was drunk, just out of it," Ian continues, shaking his head at the ground. They know he's telling the truth. James

had started drinking first thing before work for the last few days now. "He shouldn't have been up there. I just, I needed help. I needed the help so we could get out of here. I never even heard of anything like this happening. That poor dumb bastard. Jesus. Jesus Christ."

THEY HAVE NO IDEA what kind of shape James is in under all that wet concrete, but they know they'll have to dump the load somewhere and clean the huge drum. The macabre aspect of the job weighs on them.

They disengage the large, crane-like concrete pump from the bottom of the mixer and hitch the drum's trailer to the dozer. They pull the big thing on its fat, black tires to the edge of the clearing. The concrete is useless. They pour it out in a great muddy roll. It splats in sheets across fresh-smelling soil and around the trunks of black ash trees, eastern white pines, red cedars. It submerges the living sea oats and switchgrass greenery. A huge slab creeping over the earth, now freckled with hundreds and hundreds of struggling cicadas. Then out comes James, mostly still somehow sewn together, but twisted as a wet towel and cracked open in several places with big streams of his insides pulled out of him like taffy. Baxter vomits, and the other men step away from the mess, trying to hold tight to themselves inside their own minds, in their own ways, because no one wants to be like Baxter.

They rake James out of the concrete mix and onto a tarp that they fold around him. They busy themselves, spending more water than they should washing out the mixing drum. Watching the murky liquid swirl around the large blades that run through the center of the drum forces them to visualize the exact mechanics of how James died. The cicada song has grown louder every day for no imaginable reason, and now it is at a volume that would seem unattainable. Once the mixer is cleaned there's nothing left to do but talk about what happens next.

"That's it. We can't go on. We've got to get those two bodies back to the world, and I think we all need to go with them," Samuel Stern says.

All agree. As the men return to the sleeping tent to pack up their gear, they hear Ian outside trying to get the big engine on the thirteen-ton truck, which brought them in, to turn over. It moans and shakes, but it doesn't light. When Ian opens the hood he finds the engine is destroyed, encased in dead cicadas.

"Now how the fuck does that make sense to you?" Quent asks Ian as they both scan the engine. Quent turns to the gathering men. "These hoses are completely chewed through. How many bites any of you got from these damn bugs?" Victor raises his hand as if to suggest he's been bit, but Quent says, "Bullshit. It don't make no sense." He scans the faces of the men and even of Fanny who's standing away from the engine, her forehead deeply creased and her arms crossed.

"Look, I got my pickup over there," Samuel says. "That's how we came in." When they go to check the engine of the Sterns' Chevy, they find cicadas riddled through it but nothing damaged.

That only makes Quent smack his mouth and stare at the sky, bothered even more by the turn of events. "So why is one truck fucked and not the other?"

"All right," Samuel says. "We can put Homer and James in the back and me and the missus can drive into Sellersburg. It's hardly any kind of truck bed at all, but we'll rent a vehicle or get the authorities to come out and pick up the rest of you. If we leave now we might be there and back before midnight."

Ian steps forward. "Mrs. Stern, I don't mean no disrespect, but there's a real danger of the radiator overheating as the fan gets choked up with them bugs. Let me ride with Samuel. I can keep the truck in working shape."

Fanny looks at the men she'll be left behind with. She seems unsure, but before she can find her voice the others agree that at this point, taking the mechanic for the long drive back to the state road would be the smart thing to do.

They gather ragdoll James, rolled up in his tarp, and pull Homer in his blankets out of the freezer, where he's gone stiff, sculpted into a fetal position to fit the freezer's dimensions. Both bodies go in the back of the truck.

The men and Fanny watch Samuel drive slowly over the crunching cicadas toward the logging road, the tires occasionally losing purchase and spinning out on beds of bugs that provide all the traction of ice. Ian, in the passenger side of the cab, waves back at them from the window, perhaps in an effort to set their minds at ease.

As soon as the carefully lumbering pickup is out of sight, Fanny walks away from the others and back to the safety of her trailer. She aims to wash and peel potatoes, since, she tells herself, she doesn't see how Samuel can make it back before the men will need to eat. If they're delivered out of this place by sunrise it'll be a miracle. But really, of course, she just needs the work. Her mind needs it. She still feels Mac trotting next to her like a phantom limb, and now Samuel has left her here alone, save for these five strangers who stare off down the logging road even after the truck has gone. Everyone is trying to find the strength to think clearly under the persistent rapture of the cicada song, Fanny too.

It's her instinct that Baxter is harmless, and Hank has a sweetness to him that brings out the old mother in her.

Both are about the age of her own son who she hasn't seen in over a year. But the homeless man, Quent, carries a darkness about him, David Bruce a meanness, and Victor an implied violence.

She should prep the potatoes in the dining area where there's a deep, stainless steel sink, but the safety and closeness of the trailer, the scent of her man and her dog, that's what she wants. She fills a bin with water and places it right in the middle of the trailer floor. She puts another empty bowl for skinning next to it and drags in a sack of potatoes, letting in a few unwanted cicadas.

Before getting into his truck, as the other men were hurrying the heavy dead into the back, Samuel had approached Fanny with a haunted face that caused her stomach to tighten even more than it already was. But once he was sure the others couldn't see, he smiled and winked at his wife kindly and she shook her head at him, both wanting to smile herself and reproach him.

She has been deeply frightened by how things have gone since the men arrived. But Samuel was saying, without words, *I know this is all so strange. I know it's scary. I know we're sad that we lost our fine friend, Mac. But we're going to be okay.* And she too was talking without words, talking with her eyes, saying to him, *Don't be gone long. Something's not right here.* They were just children when they first met, and despite the years that have passed, in private, they can still be childish with each other in all the best ways.

She washes and peels too many potatoes while sitting there on the floor of the trailer. She stares out the screen window as her hands work. The screens are covered in wriggling cicadas. So dense is their cluster that they keep most of the sunlight from coming in. She's turned on the trailer's little yellow bulbs in their tiny shades, casting a dim glow that doesn't reach the darkened corners.

"Something's not right," she says out loud now, telling the

potatoes as she carves away at them. Images of Homer's life-less face, mouth agape; James's tarp-wrapped form; or Mac's lean, limp body spilled in eternal surrender occasionally rise, unwanted, to the front of her thoughts despite the busywork.

It's a little over two hours later when she hears commotion from David Bruce, and then from the other men, outside the trailer. She has since finished the potatoes and only now realizes that she's been staring at nothing at all, lost in the haze of the insect song. For how long she can't say. The yells of the men outside bring her back to herself. The light in the trailer has darkened, and she's only noticing it now. Through the obstructed screen she can see Victor and Hank running toward the logging road. Her heart begins to beat faster.

She emerges into fading, coral daylight to see the men gathered. Beyond them is Ian, the little mechanic, on foot. No truck. No Samuel. Ian's tightly buttoned vest is caked with something. His eyes are wild and frightened. He walks like his body has been knocked crooked, like a giant fist has clenched itself around him. He rubs his neck with his hand, pained.

Fanny begins to run toward the shambling Ian. He grows larger in her vision. Clearer. His round face, horrified by what he's seen, is lacerated. She can see that now. She can see that it's blood that's caked across his vest.

He stumbles into camp with big, red-eyed bugs in his hair, causing her to realize his tweed flat cap is missing. She catches up to the cluster of men. Ian is saying something he can barely get out but knows he must. He's animated by the opposing forces of panic and fatigue, sadness and fear.

He stammers, "W-we were going too fast. The road must be inches deep with those bugs . . ." His words land against Fanny like waves on rocks. "Samuel . . . he lost control. We slid down a hill. We hit a tree real, real hard on the driver's side. A branch came in . . . he . . . he's dead . . . Samuel's dead . . ."

Fanny's wretched scream saps all of her strength. She looks as if she's about to fall. Victor moves to catch her but she pushes him away and stays on her feet, swaying, bellowing, "Don't touch me!"—her face like crumpled pink paper. She repeats Ian's words to him—"Lost control?"—as if Ian is telling her that he has seen the actual devil out in the woods. As if he's asking her to believe in something that simply cannot be.

"No, no, no . . ." Quent says forcibly, his words tumbling out. "Hold the fuck on!" He glowers at Ian with large eyes, searching carefully for something in Ian's frightened face. Everyone waits for Quent's next words, hoping he can make sense of things for them, but instead Quent goes silent, holding on to something he can't articulate. He starts to rock back and forth from one foot to the other.

"You . . . you okay, Ian?" Baxter asks. The little mechanic doesn't answer but seems to give it real consideration, like Baxter's question is the first he's thought of himself at all. He looks frail before the other men, with his small stature and his shaken aura. There is a heat coming off the group.

Done searching for words, Quent screams out, hoping to be louder than the cicadas' constant song, "This is fucking insane!"

"Take me to him! Take me to Samuel!" Fanny yells at Ian. She gathers up the other men in her gaze. "What if he's still alive? We have to get him. We have to get out of this horrible place!"

"The walk. The bugs. You can't imagine it," Ian tells her, his voice quivering.

Quent stares at the ground, at his own shifting feet, and says, "First light tomorrow, I'm walking out. I'm done. That's it!"

Fanny doesn't let Quent finish. She steps on his words. She barks, "No! No! I'm going to see Samuel now! Which one of you sons-of-bitches is going to help me?"

"Mrs. Stern. I'm so, so sorry . . . Samuel is dead, I-I saw

it . . ." Ian has pools of empathy welling in his eyes. "There's nothing we can do right now."

Fanny walks wide around Ian, as though he takes up more space than he actually does, crunching bugs as she marches off toward the logging road. "That's what you all said about Homer! We are not handling Samuel that way!"

Hank runs after Fanny. "Mrs. Stern, wait, please . . . just, hold on now. It's, it's getting dark, there's not going to be any moon out tonight . . . we've got to . . ." The song drones on all around them.

Hank keeps talking to Fanny, using a calm, kind voice and rare compassion. He manages to keep her from heading farther down the logging road after Samuel, but he doesn't manage to turn her around. The two stand there for some time, until it's dark enough that they look like ghosts.

IV

VI

IT MIGHT BE past midnight. Everybody is still awake. They've been eating canned beans, not wanting to bother Fanny for dinner. But now there are sounds coming from inside the Sterns' trailer.

Fanny is inside, banging pots and slamming the stove door. Ian calls out to the trailer, telling her she doesn't have to work for them any more, but Hank touches Ian's arm gently. "Leave her be for a while."

Twenty minutes later Fanny emerges from her trailer carrying a large tin platter of food. She drops the platter down on the long wooden table in front of the men, who suddenly lurch away from her. The platter is heaped with steaming, cooked cicadas, stirred with canola oil and salt and pepper, roasted in the oven until well-browned.

The men are startled and suddenly nervous, except for Victor, who almost laughs, holding his ground on the bench.

David Bruce is wide-eyed. "Woman? What in the Sam Hill? Have you gone hysterical?" His voice is angry and devoid of pity. To him she seems almost amused, scoffing at him with her eyes. He raises his hand as if to strike her, but it's only a momentary reaction. His intentions wither under her

gaze and that of the other men. His hand falls back to his side.

Every living human soul in the camp settles into silence, sitting or standing over the tin platter of sizzling, browned cicadas.

"Quent?"

Quent had palmed Homer's tobacco when the others were wrapping his body in blankets several days ago, and now he's standing off alone near the sunken shelter construction, smoking with one hand and sloshing what's left of James's whiskey down his throat with the other. He is working hard at devouring the vices of the dead. He is trying to think, but the cicada song is pervasive. There's no clarity inside of it. So he's doing this instead.

"Quent!"

He thinks he hears his name. He spins, jumpy, the whiskey sloshing in its flask. It wouldn't be the first time he's heard things in the song that weren't there. But it's real. Someone's approaching, silhouetted against the distant lights of the dining area. It is Ian, still limping from the accident.

"Quent? I need to talk to you."

Quent sucks the hand-rolled down to a tiny roach. He holds the smoke as deep in the depths of him as he can, desperate for it to fill him and replace his suffocating worry. Every night since they first arrived he has dreamed of his father. *So talk*, he means to say, but it's more important to keep the hot smoke inside, so he just nods at Ian the mechanic to go ahead.

"I saw how you were about the chewed-through hoses on the rig. I didn't want to tell the others because, because I don't even know what's what, but I think, and maybe this is best kept between us, but . . ."

The anxiety Quent came here to escape is mounting. He's nodding his head as if still acknowledging Ian, but really he's nodding to some hidden rhythm inside the insect song. It's a struggle to listen past it.

"At the accident today, I thought about what you said, about these bugs not biting us. So I, I managed to get the hood of Samuel's truck open after, after we sideswiped that tree. I mean, it was all bent to shit, but . . ."

Quent nods and struggles to pull more smoke from the roach.

"I think, I think someone might have messed with Samuel's brakes."

Quent nods again.

"I found small cuts in the lines. Not, not like on the big truck. Not obvious, but just where the lines take the most pressure, someone had . . . someone had maybe compromised them, Quent. I mean, I think. I don't . . . " Quent continues nodding. ". . . know for sure. The brakes didn't burst. It was Samuel, he damn well lost control on the road, and honestly, I don't blame him. You don't know what it's like out there. So . . . I don't . . ." Ian begins to nod in time with Quent as the two men stare at each other. Ian starts to repeat himself, uncertain of whether Quent is even comprehending him. "It's just, with the big truck's engine the way it was and how you said something about it, I thought I could trust you. And maybe I'm wrong. Maybe I'm talking a bunch of flimflam and I'm just . . . going funny, 'cause of . . ." Ian blinks tiredly. "Of everything that's happened . . ." Then he stops talking and stops nodding along.

Quent keeps nodding. He makes one last attempt at a drag, burning the tips of his fingers, and throws what's left away. He tilts more whiskey into him, recklessly swallowing, until he finds the will to speak. "Okay, since it's just speculation, I ain't gonna tell the others. This is just between you and me. But I'm walking out of here tomorrow and that's all there is to it. You can come with me. Everyone can come. We'll all walk out together. That's probably for the best. And when we get into town you can tell the authorities your . . . you know, what's on your mind. And that's all there is."

Ian nods. "Okay. Okay, Quent. That's the plan then. But listen. I keep trying to tell everyone what it's like. It's real hard out there. It's different out there."

After the men have gone to bed and all the lights in the camp are off, Fanny sits alone in the trailer. The large bowl of raw, skinned potatoes is still in the middle of the floor. The night is dark, the trailer darker because of the bug-clotted screens blocking out the starlight.

Over the last few hours she has wept and screamed and broken things and pressed her face against the pillow where Samuel lay his head and put dog food in Mac's bowl that he will never eat. Now she's sitting on the bed, staring at nothing again, listening to the male cicadas wail. Listening to the song open and expand and breathe all around her.

Then, as clear as if she had snapped her own fingers, she hears Samuel's voice outside on the logging road, enmeshed in the song.

"Fanny! Fanny, honey! Fanny, I need your help!"

She bolts out of the trailer like that was the only thing in the world she was waiting to hear. Like Samuel's voice is a starting gun. She huffs across the land of living bugs, her footing careless.

"Samuel?" she calls into the night.

"Fanny, I need you!"

"I'm coming!" she cries out. "I'm coming!"

But now someone is behind her, an ungainly form, running with her toward the logging road. Is the form chasing her or coming to help with Samuel? Samuel is ahead of her and the form is behind her. But now she can't hear Samuel's voice. She can't see Samuel as she closes in on the logging road. It occurs to her that she might have imagined hearing him. The song does such strange things to your mind. Her foot slips on mashed cicadas. Her ankle rolls and she falls hard, skipping against the ground. Then the form is on her, a large rock in its hand.

It holds her down atop the field of cicadas. Fanny can feel them beneath her, writhing like hundreds of fingers, being crushed, struggling to live. Everything is always struggling to live. The heavy rock comes down on her face so that she feels her own skull give way above her nose. Soap pours into her eyes, like when she's in the shower. But no, it's not soap. It's blood, and there's a blinding, searing white light coming from behind her eyes. It's a man. One of the fucking men is on top of her. Beating her. That's the only thing she knows. She can no longer see. Her thoughts are blowing apart. The pain subsumes her.

The man is going to bring the rock down on her a second time. She means to grab at his forearms, or to block her face, or to do anything at all that might save her, but her hands don't follow her commands, and her body is seizing beneath her assailant's weight.

A cool breeze blows through the opening in her skull. Cicadas are already hopping into the wet cavity. When the man brings the rock down on her a second time he smashes some of the bugs into her already-cracked skull.

Fanny is ejected out of her body by the force of the second blow. She sails away on the cicada song, tumbling into the searing light that has now expanded to engulf all things. There's a dark spot at the center of the white light, a deep black dot, and she flies toward it, falling inside of it, inside of its blackness. Swallowed by it. The black dot is a well now, and that's where she drowns.

I T'S VICTOR who finds Mrs. Stern come daylight. He's walking the perimeter of the camp, thinking about death and
the unfamiliar land they've found themselves in. Thinking
about the people he's let down over the span of his life, about
how he got here, to this place, the poor decisions he's made,
the roughness he's relied on to define himself for so long.
About how much of it comes from an overwhelming, early
need to simply survive, and how, over time, that struggle has
made him coarse. He wishes he could talk to Hank more,
make a friend of the boy, maybe find something stupid and
meaningless to laugh about together. But all Hank wants to
talk about is Victor's fighting days, and that's not something
Victor wants to drag up out here, or anywhere really. These
are the things on his mind when he first sees her, face down,
planted hard against a rock some forty feet ahead of him,
brains and skull bits shimmering with cicadas and ants. The
earth around her head soaked with blood.

"Aw, hell! Aw, Jesus!" Victor yells out. He presses his hands
against the sides of his head, trying to cradle his brain, protect
it. He has to stand near the body longer than he'd like, calling
out for the others before they, weary of surprises, join him.

Hank, who had been the most kind toward Mrs. Stern last night, sinks a little when he sees her. His shoulders lose their density and he shuts his eyes tight, lifts his hands to pull at his own black hair now long since gone wild. "What is happening?" he cries.

Ian, his vest still stained with blood from yesterday's car accident, is the most appalled. Victor watches him turn away as if to bolt. Of all the men, Ian has seen the most since these deaths began. His endurance for it seems to be waning fast.

David Bruce looks more confused than stricken. "Did she . . . did she trip? On these bugs? She was so crazy last night. She must've lost it and—"

He doesn't get to finish before Quent grabs him by his shirt and starts to shake him. "Where the fuck were you last night?" Baxter, who is closest to them, stumbles from the sudden conflict so fast he ends up falling on his ass in the bugs.

David Bruce clumsily yanks himself free of Quent. "Get off! The hell you sweating me for?"

There are things Quent's been thinking, things he hasn't said, and some of those things come out now in a rush as he points a shaking finger at David Bruce. "Somebody put something in Homer's coffee! I saw Mac drink from that same cup and neither one of those poor bastards lived through the night! Now Mrs. Stern has slipped and fallen so hard that her goddamned skull is scattered all over the ground? That's a bunch of bullshit!"

The men stare at Quent and David Bruce, six of them in total now. David Bruce is shocked by the accusations. "You're crazy, Quent! I was on my cot in that tent with the rest of you all night long. I mean, what are you even accusing me of? Why would I do this? That woman was going mad! You saw her! We all saw her! She did this to herself, I'm telling you."

Victor glares down at David Bruce. "You seem keen on convincing us this was an accident. Looked like you was ready to hit her last night. You into that? You like hitting women?"

David Bruce spits on the ground and snarls at Victor. "You fucking nigg—" Victor puts his left fist squarely into the facial pocket just below David Bruce's cheekbone so fast that it seems as if he's been cocked to do it since he met the man. He hits so hard that David Bruce's knees turn to water beneath him and he crumbles.

David Bruce is on the ground now, conscious but confused about where he is for maybe fifteen seconds while his feet bicycle against the ground, vying for traction among the cicadas. Victor holds his stance as David Bruce struggles to stand. None of the men try to help him or to contain Victor. Victor knows he only needs to hit David Bruce one time for the man to fall into line, and so he doesn't move on him again. David Bruce, slowly standing, has nothing left to say. He presses his hand to his jaw.

Quent backs off, knowing he's planted a seed of violence that's bloomed here in the hard morning light. "That's it. I don't know what's going on, but I'm—we're—walking out! Together! Right now! Like we said last night! When we get to civilization we'll send the heat back here to work all this through. And I swear to God, if any of you are against that idea, I'll leave you here." No one disagrees. No one mentions that last night it was just Quent walking out, and now come morning he's ordering them all on the march. No one looks like they mind that Quent, the least skilled and sound among them, has taken control.

They don't even cover Mrs. Stern. Quent says it could be a crime scene, though even he doesn't look like he's entirely sure of that anymore, despite the drama he started over her body. They return to the sleeping tent to grab their packs. David Bruce, his face beginning to swell, clips his handgun in its holster to his belt. All the men notice this, but Victor holds his eyes on David Bruce's gun the longest.

"I'm not going to shoot you for sucker punching me, boy.

Don't worry," David Bruce says to Victor, his grin already lopsided from the inflammation.

"Can't help but notice the first man to call me 'boy' since we got out here waited until he strapped on a piece to do it," Victor says, his face hard as stone.

Many at odds with one another, they all begin walking down the logging road.

The logging road runs south, maybe. It's hard to say once the men are under the trees and the road begins to twist. Their faces are wrapped. Their hats are pulled low, save for Ian, whose cap has been missing since the accident. They wear long pants and long sleeves. The cicadas bang away at their covered mouths, wanting inside of them.

Away from the clearing, surrounded by the wooded thicket, the extent of the emergence is awe inspiring. It's hard to fully grasp the density of cicadas, flying, chanting, crawling, fucking, living incomprehensible lives. The men are already tired under the persistence and volume of the bugs always on them, always underneath their feet, voices always in their ears, bodies always flapping against their hands. So alive with bugs are the woods that nature has become a single, tottering thing. The green around the men is thinner than when they first rolled down this road, in the process of being consumed by a million tiny, gnawing mouths.

Yesterday's blood on Ian's vest has gone black like hardened ink. Baxter, walking behind Ian, wonders why he hasn't taken the vest off, considering its state and the summer heat. Ian, limping badly from the accident, suffering silently among the men, seems the most frayed of them all, and that's something Baxter can understand.

Eventually they see Samuel's truck. It slid sideways down an incline and is wedged up on the driver's side among some trees. Victor and Quent begin to make their way down to it. Ian tells them he can't stand to see it again and he steps back from the sight, his hands up, warding the truck off like an evil spirit.

The bed is empty. Tangled out in the woods beyond are the two bodies, tossed in the impact. Inside the cab lifeless Samuel stares past the bugs swarming his face and out of the broken front windshield into the infinite crawl. Samuel stares at everything, endlessly surprised, forever alarmed. It's hard to see much detail with the swarm of bugs jostling over the surface of the corpse, but Samuel's throat seems to have been gouged fiercely, and there's a lot of dried blood spray in the cab. Ian's cap is crumpled down beneath Samuel's feet. Victor tries to say something to Quent about the state of Samuel's body, but the horny, screeching, clacking male chorus is louder here by the Chevy than Victor has heard it anywhere else since the song began. It's deafening to him now, piercing, and he has to cover his ears with his hands.

Victor helps Quent struggle back up the slope to the logging road where the others have been staring down at them. It isn't easy. Both of them now carry yet another sight in their heads they wish they'd never seen.

The men press on down the logging road but the bulk of cicadas and the decibel level of their song exhausts everyone. David Bruce, his cheek now properly swollen and blackening, finally yells out above the din to the others, "I'm going back. The clearing was different. Different from this. There's food and water back there. I mean, how much longer does this last with these bugs? Couple of weeks? We can wait it out. This don't feel right out here. Something's off."

The others stop walking. They all want to turn back but no one says it. Instead, Quent says, "I knew it would be you."

"Now you cut that shit out, Quent! I mean it, how long did we ride on this road?" David Bruce asks. "Ian, you were driving. You know where we are."

"It's about fifty-five, sixty miles out of these woods to the main highway. We can do it before dawn if we press on after nightfall, but not at the rate we're walking now." Ian has to yell above the song to be heard.

David Bruce turns back toward the clearing. "Yeah, I ain't doing it. We've been walking for an hour and I already feel like my brain is vibrating out of my noggin. No way. Come for me when you get help."

Victor, as if looking for an excuse to punch David Bruce again but also being very aware of his handgun, says, "'Cause you're the killer. That's why you don't want us to get out of this place. You wanna go back and hide the evidence of what you've done to Mrs. Stern. Or you wanna pick us off one by one."

"I could just shoot you now! How am I a killer, Victor? How does that work?" The way David Bruce yells at Victor, with his hand casually resting on his gun, makes everyone nervous, not just Victor. "What killer? Because this hobo, Quent, says there's a killer that just makes it so? Did you see how fucking drunk Quent was last night? Or how about this, did you see how Hank was trying to get into Widow Stern's pants, her husband not even cold? Being all bullshit nice to her. Maybe he paid her a visit and she wasn't having it and it all went south! How about that for a theory?"

Hank starts walking toward David Bruce with a mighty and sudden intent. "You are a piece of shit!" he yells over the song. "You are a piece of fucking shit!"

"Hey! Watch yourself!" David Bruce yells back at Hank, leveling a hand at him to stay his advance, but not the one he's resting on his gun. Hank stops, but his glare is poisonous and his breathing is hard. "There's a whole lot of fucking maybes is all I'm saying," David Bruce growls, then turns and begins walking to the clearing. "Can't you people see? We're all going crazy out here," he calls back at them. "If any of you think this is something more than a horrible, nightmare coincidence then you're the dangerous ones. God took Fanny and Samuel and James and Homer so they wouldn't have to be in this mess with you assholes," he says, his final words drowned out by the song.

Tacitly, without further discussion, they all turn back in the direction of the clearing. Even Quent does so without much internal fight, though he sulks for the others to witness. As they walk back to the construction site the cicadas seem to relent, even just a little, and their chorus turns toward a more tolerable bass and away from the sharp whining it had taken on as the men pushed deeper into the woods.

"We can start a fire when we get back," Hank says to Quent as they walk. "A big one, but controlled. Maybe some fire-watch will see it and send a plane to investigate."

The plans for the bomb shelter call for grenade and flood sumps to be dug five feet down in front of the main entrance and also at the smaller rear hatch. The metal doors have yet to be affixed, but the sumps have been dug and set with concrete and masonry. Hank uses the dozer to bring over four sixty-gallon diesel drums, and Quent and Ian pour the fuel from the drums into the front entrance sump. The oily liquid is the color of urine and flows out thick, splashing back on them, slick to the touch. Baxter, David Bruce, and Victor hack unused wood into transportable pieces and carry them to the sump to sink in with the diesel. Hank takes a gas metal arc welder and David Bruce a propane torch, and they start blasting the surface of the oily pool, trying to force a cycle of evaporation that will lead to a sustainable burn. The bits of lumber breaking the surface catch immediately. Eventually, with some difficulty, the surface begins to belch short, orange plumes in patches where the men pour on the heat and flame. They practically have to light each individual foot of the pool by hand. Then, once most of the sump is lit, the heat at the rim of it quickly becomes intolerable and Hank and David Bruce have to retreat, but the job is done.

The sump burn is infernal. The substrate of the burn,

where the surface of the diesel pool meets the air, is a rich orange, like the veins in cicada wings, like the sky the day dead James received the starlings. The orange reaches less than a few feet into the air before it transforms into a thick black velvet billow, lifting in a wide, drifting column that would be impossible to miss for miles from above the treetops. The men throw more lumber into the sump until the heat makes the entire concoction unapproachable. The thermal waves are so thick they cast rolling vapor shadows on the ground around the fire. Most of the cicadas move in throngs away from the radiating heat, but some, panicked and damned by the chaos, leap into the fire, ending instantly in tiny pops.

The men stand transfixed by the black, hot fire from whatever distance each feels comfortable. Finally, reluctantly, Hank announces that he can't leave Mrs. Stern sprawled and exposed anymore, so he and Victor drift off toward the logging road to take care of it.

The two men sweep as many cicadas off of Fanny as they can and brush ants from her clothes but not from her head, where they swarm and glint. Victor and Hank lay a tarp out next to her body. Victor takes her wrists and Hank takes her ankles. When they lift, Fanny's head falls forward and black slop spills from her skull. Victor looks up at the blue sky and takes a breath. "Goddamn it," he says.

They carry her over to the tarp and lay her, nice and easy, facedown. They wrap and tie her into a package. "Fuck," Hank says, and it looks like he's about to cry. His eyes water but he shuts them tight against the tears. They carry the Fanny package to the freezer where they'd kept Homer until yesterday and shut her inside the sharp coldness.

The sump fire seems to be burning the day away because dusk comes sooner than it should, and then night falls heavy and fast around them. Perhaps because the men have had trouble turning away from the fire, and their eyes have grown tight

against its light. The subtlety of the day's changes have been lost to them. Baxter looks the most spellbound by the fire. Quent recognizes the sallow-eyed boy's stare from the night they both looked out over the woods together and he talked about the ocean.

Baxter says, "It's like Gehenna." Quent nods, not because he knows what Gehenna is, he doesn't, but because it seemed about time for Baxter to say something bat-shit crazy. "The constant burning trash dump in the bible, you know?" Baxter asks the men, as if they're a pack of seminarians. "Where all the filth and dead of the world are tossed. Where people went to sacrifice their children."

David Bruce shakes his head at Baxter. "Son, I read my bible every goddamned day. I never heard of that."

But Baxter doesn't register the dissent. "I haven't seen you open your bible once since we've been here." Before David Bruce can snap back, Baxter is moving on. "We're in Hell. I bet we're all murderers or rapists or thieves or something. I bet we're already dead and this is Hell."

David Bruce doesn't like this talk. He shakes his head. "You don't know anything about Hell."

Hank, not turning from the light, finally starts to cry, having been on the verge of it since he lay hands on dead Mrs. Stern. The tears dry fast from the fire's heat. "I got another fella killed on a work site in Chicago two years back. I wasn't paying attention. I'd been partying the night before. I was in rough shape. I shouldn't have been working, but I needed the money. I caught him between a wall and the treads of the backhoe I was driving. I didn't even hear his screams. Just tore him all up. I lost everything. I've been knocking around looking for off-book, non-union work ever since. But I, I guess maybe I ain't lost enough yet. A man's life seems like an expensive thing, so . . ."

No one stares at the other, all stare into the fire. Only the spewing, black diesel smoke exists. Victor sucks in the oily, sweet air. "I ran over a little girl while I was drunk. And I-I kept driving. I knew she was dead too. I saw it in the papers the next day. I never got caught. Never won another fight after, neither. Got lost in my head. Just got lost." The fire burns.

"I'm a faggot," Baxter says.

David Bruce turns strained and glassy eyes toward Baxter, as if this is the worst thing he's heard tonight. "You filthy, pervert piece of trash. I swear, if you ever so much as look at me again, I will kill you."

Baxter is unafraid. "I told you. We're already dead."

Some cicadas leap into the fire, most don't. Their song shakes the world, louder than even the roar of the burn. Ian is silent. Quent is so close to the fire that he's drenched in sweat from its heat. No one seems to even register the crimes of Hank and Victor.

Quent thinks that he could tell the other men about his father now. His looming, dark force of a father who was always either beating on young Quent or pressing his drunk self against Quent's little, frightened body in dreamlike, late-night visitations to his bedroom. Quent could maybe talk about how his father broke him so bad that Quent can't stay in one place, can't find affection in the arms of women or men because, whatever he's attracted to, he feels the urge to beat the shit out of. How he has trouble sleeping through the night because down in the deepest place of rest is where his father still lives. He could tell them how he would take his own life if he didn't have such a strong will to live, and how this need to both live and die creates a push and pull on his soul that he knows will one day rip him in two. It seems like the moment for it. Like for once in his life he could say these things out loud, like he and these other men are all part of a Neolithic tribe performing a group exorcism at the foot of some sacred light, some burning bush. But if he says it out loud it means that either Baxter is right and a divine force has brought all

these evil men together to be punished or that every man in the whole world is just a broken shell, a billion discarded, meaningless, fragile, nymph casings. So he says nothing at all.

Cicada-fat bats drunkenly flap in and out of the fire's glow. David Bruce starts to talk, and maybe he too has something to confess. But instead he says, "I have to take a shower and change my clothes or I'm going to go nuts. I got a lot of that diesel on me and it never does lose its sense of slime. Hey, Baxter, don't you get no ideas and try to come spy on me while I'm in there, you hear me."

Baxter, still living in a past conversation, says, "I was raised in a Pentecostal tent-church in LaFollette, Tennessee. My people worship God by handling poisonous serpents. My parents would kill me if they knew my urges. Literally kill me. You tell me I don't know God, don't know God's cruelty, don't know God's idea of Hell. You tell me that reading your bible in between bouts of screwing whores means you know more about grace lost than I do. Go fuck yourself, you blind-ass, hypocritical shit heel."

David Bruce erupts at this, suddenly deeply pained, screaming back at Baxter, "I ain't never screwed no whores!" To Quent it sounds like Baxter just hurt David Bruce as much as Victor did this morning with his left hook.

The men are prairies apart from one another in all but distance. Quent, Hank, Victor, and Baxter stay by the fire. Quent shares Homer's tobacco with Victor and Hank silently. Baxter stands off alone, his arms wrapped around himself. Ian and David Bruce float off to the group sleeping tent. In the tent David Bruce grabs fresh clothes and a towel, all recently hand-laundered and sun-dried on the line by Mrs. Stern, and heads out to the wooden stall showers by the latrines. He hangs his belt with his handgun in its clip-on holster and his other clothes on a hook, and then relishes in the lazy wash of day-warmed water from the gravity shower. After a good scrubbing he exits to find his .45 gone, only the empty holster and clothes remaining.

In a panic, clean clothes sticking to his wet body, David Bruce returns to the signal fire. The only men he finds there now are Victor and Quent. "Where the fuck's my gun! You take my gun, you Negro son-of-a-bitch?"

"You're awfully mouthy for a man who just lost his one strength in the world," Victor says, turning his shoulders toward David Bruce so he can come at the man square if he must.

But Quent is alert to the possibilities. "Hold on, someone in this camp stole your gun?"

"You two were both here? The whole time?" David Bruce asks. He looks like a wild man in the roaring, fire-lit night.

Quent turns to Victor. "Naw, Victor went back to the dining tent."

"To eat, motherfucker!" Victor yells.

David Bruce sticks his narrow eyes to Victor. "And you were with James when he fell into that mixer too!"

"I was nowhere near the man! I'm telling you! You all know he was piss drunk when he fell in!" Victor's starting to feel it. *The press.* When shit goes bad for a honky, people who look like him take the brunt of it. That's what Victor calls *the press.* "And you better drop that look, Quent! How do I know you've been at this fire the whole time?"

David Bruce wants an inventory of all the living. "Fine, so where's Hank? Where's Baxter? They off playing fiddly-dicks with each other somewhere? Where's Ian?"

Quent scans the clearing. The large earth movers loom in the firelight, casting long, whipping shadows where a man could easily hide. "I, I don't know. I don't know where anyone is."

David Bruce scans the area now too with the concern of a superstitious man in a land of ghosts. "You know something,

Quent. You were right, one of you is a goddamned killer, and now he's got my gun."

Ian has carried the radio from the dining area to the sleeping tent. He sits outside the front door of the large tent cradling the mechanism in his arms. He seems to have surrendered the idea of pushing away the cicadas that crawl over him and has instead taken to enduring them. Without the tin-strainer antenna the signal is scratchy and crackling.

Senator McCarthy is attacking former president, Truman, for questioning his practices. McCarthy is celebrating the honesty of FBI Director Hoover. McCarthy is telling America that it is riddled with people who want to undo their country, masticate it from the inside. That it's an invasion, an assault on our national freedoms.

David Bruce, Quent, and Victor approach Ian to ask about the missing handgun. Ian doesn't seem fully present, but he eventually manages to stammer that he has no idea where the gun is. Hank and Baxter are inside the tent, and now that all the men are in one place, David Bruce runs another round of accusations. "You talked a bunch of weird shit to me earlier, you sick fuck!" he yells at Baxter. "You gonna take me out with my own gun? Like you cut the brakes on Samuel's truck! Like you beat Fanny to death!" Baxter stares back at David Bruce coldly.

Quent, surprised at the mention of cut brakes, looks to Ian. Ian still seems dazed, holding the horrid, crackling radio to his chest. No one but the mechanic and Quent should know anything about any compromised brakes. Quent pulls his gaze from Ian and says to the tent, "We should all stay together until someone comes to check on our signal fire and gets us out of here. Whatever is going on, it's got to stop. Nobody else is going to die." And like so many of the plans the men have made, none agree using their words but all agree nonetheless.

* * *

They lie on their cots. The diesel fire is out there in the night, exhaling, casting its glow into the large tent through the screen windows. The cicada chorus hums in tune with the fire's roar. Quent's sleep is cursed. He dreams that his father is stalking the camp. A silhouetted figure with no face.

The men have each hung tarps and burlap and sheets and blankets up around their beds to create makeshift, mostly opaque bug nets that don't always work at keeping stray cicadas off of them while they sleep. In this enclosed, oneiric space Quent hears a distant gunshot. He stirs. He opens his eyes. He listens. The sump fire. The insect chorus. Then another gunshot. It's not a dream. He pulls the thick hanging blanket that isolates his cot back to look around at the flickering tent. Hank, Ian, Baxter, and Victor are gone. David Bruce is the only one still there and he's already on his feet staring back at Quent. David Bruce whispers, "That's my gun."

The two men don't move for a moment. They wait for a third discharge, but it doesn't come. Finally, they gather their courage and head outside.

Victor is outside the tent door, dragging hard on the last of a cigarette.

"You hear that?" Quent asks.

Victor tosses his cigarette on the ground and points calmly to the dining area. "It came from over there. Where's everyone else?"

Quent is pissed and scared. "We were all supposed to stay together!"

"So, what now?" David Bruce asks, looking from Quent's face to Victor's. "We going over there or . . . ?"

Small amounts of time pass in big arcs, then Victor says, "What the fuck else we gonna do?"

Inside the dark dining area, tented off by tarps, Ian the

mechanic and Hank the heavy machinery operator are dead. Both men have been shot. Ian has been shot in the head, between the eyes and from a slightly tilted angle, so that a cone of red chunks bow out from the exit wound, splash across the dining table and plaster up the tarp wall. His stained vest is torn open with several buttons missing. Larger, younger Hank looks like he put up even more of a fight against the killer, having taken a clumsy bullet from up underneath his chin. He's slouched on the dirt floor of the dining area, legs spread comically, with his back propped against the bench seat and his shattered jaw dangling from the still-connected tissue, ribbons of gore spilling down the front of him like a glistening bib.

Sallow-eyed Baxter is the only man alive who's not in the dining area.

"I fucking knew it was the queer all along," David Bruce says. His voice is shaking but certain.

Victor shuffles his feet, feeling as if he's coming undone, like he can't be still or he'll fall into pieces right here in front of the others. His shifting boot strikes something heavy on the ground. The clack of it draws all three men's attention. David Bruce's handgun is at Victor's feet. Tossed aside. The men stare at it. The black metal seems to absorb what little light is in the dining area. The gun sags heavy against the earth, like a rock on a pillow. David Bruce moves fast to grab it but the distance for Victor is shorter and straight down, and the gun finds its way into his hand first.

"I'm keeping it," Victor says. It's obvious this doesn't sit right with David Bruce, but he doesn't say anything. He's quivering like it's freezing, though the night is warm. He steps back, raising his hands as if he expects Victor to start shooting right then and there. Victor says, "We need to find the fairy and keep him on lock down 'til we figure out what to do next," as if the dusty gun is a totem of leadership.

The three walk into the night to find Baxter. Quent drags

a long steel pipe wrench from one of the workbenches and it clanks at his side, comforting him as they search.

VI

IV

BAXTER LOOKS LIKE one of Hank's folded monte cards. He is bent over and caught on the concrete frame of the burning sump, draped so that half of his form is still in the fire and half is hanging into the mostly constructed bomb shelter where the descending concrete entrance steps have been set. Victor, Quent, and David Bruce have to get as close as they can to the signal fire to see if it's really him burning in the liquid pit or just some debris caught in the blaze. They get so close that the thermal wind from the fire brushes their hair and ripples their clothes.

Baxter is blackened and horrible and long past dead, his charred body an interlocutor between the three living men and the hard, sudden truth that they were wrong about Baxter. The killer in the camp can now only be one of them. One of them has shot Ian and Hank and thrown Baxter to his death in the burning sump.

The insect chorus is shaking the whole universe. Distant stars are blasting apart like dandelions in the wind before the rolling song. It would not surprise any of the three men if the night sky shattered above their heads, proving all along it was only made of painted glass.

VII

DAVID BRUCE STARTS WALKING BACKWARD, all of his attention on Victor. "Get away from him, Quent!"

Victor looks confused, out of sorts. The gun dangles heavy at the end of his hanging arm, the barrel pointed at the ground lazily.

"Just . . . just hold on now! Hold on!" Quent says.

"Victor wasn't inside the tent with us when we heard the gunshots," David Bruce calls. "He's strong enough to throw Baxter into the fire. He could've done that anytime while we were sleeping. He rigged the brakes on Samuel's truck. He poisoned Homer. He beat Mrs. Stern to death, killed that poor Christian woman in cold blood with his bare monkey hands. And he says he wasn't nowhere near James when he fell into that mixer, but where was he then? Do you remember? I sure as hell don't!"

Farther and farther away from the fire David Bruce is walking, backward, keeping his eyes on Victor, looking for some darkness to hide himself in. The space between him and Victor is snowing with flying cicadas.

"Wait!" Quent says, trying hard to think next to the fire and under the weight of the cicada song while also moving slowly away from Victor, circling to the big man's left side, the large pipe wrench still in his hand. "Let's . . . let's suss all this out now. Why would Victor throw away the gun after he shot Ian and Hank?"

Victor notices the two men are talking about him like he's not even there now, even though he is at the center of their attentions.

"To avoid suspicion, goddamn it!" David Bruce cries out, because the distance between them is growing and the chorus and the fire are hard to hear over. "He knew exactly where it was in the dining area. He left it there. He ran back to the sleeping tent and he waited for us to come outside so we could go with him. See him find it. To make us drop our guard. Shit, I don't know!"

Now Victor is looking down at the gun in his hand. "Why would I? Why would I kill people like that?" he asks the gun.

"Why the hell would anyone do any of this?" David Bruce cries, still backing away.

"No . . . no, I ain't no killer."

"You killed that little girl! You admitted to it!"

"I ain't THE killer!" Victor yells, and now he's looking up at David Bruce.

Victor is an apparition before the burning fire. His complexion swallowed in the orange light. For the first time since he was awoken by gunshots, Quent remembers dreaming about his father, a dark figure, stalking the camp. Quent calls to Victor from Victor's left, where he's standing now, "Victor, if you ain't the killer, just throw the gun in the fire. We'll stay together until someone finds us. Let's let the authorities work through all of this."

Victor sees the two men, one moving away from him, the other circling him carefully, both of them beaming with fear. All three of them bathed in the song and the fire's heat. Victor feels *the press*. There's no way he won't get the blame for all of this. Gleefully, back in the world, they'll report about the

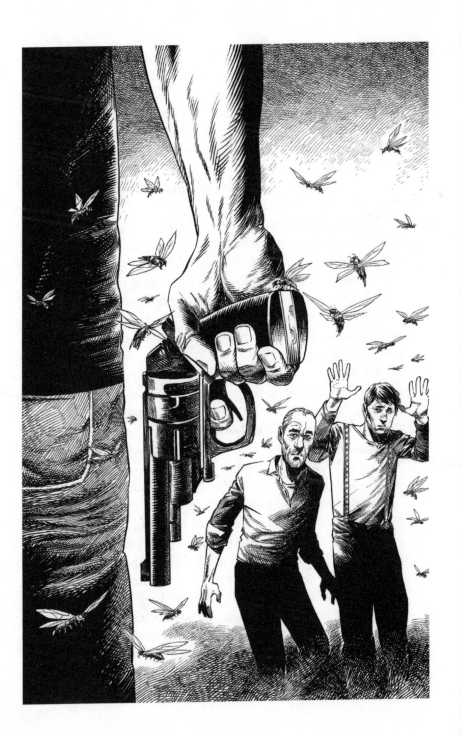

seven people and the dog the ex-boxer killed. And maybe it'll be right, not truthful, but right, some spiritual payback for the death of that poor little girl so long ago.

David Bruce breaks into a run, his back to Victor and Quent now. He's angling for cover behind the parked dozer across the clearing. "I ain't sticking around to get murdered by this maniac!" he calls back, but there is the diesel fire and the insect chorus, and his words are small in comparison to everything else around them.

Victor understands. He's going to take the rap for something one of these two white men have done. Something unimaginable. The mental calculation doesn't take long. Is the murderer Quent the hobo, who never once said a dehumanizing thing to him? Or is it the man who brought the gun into this damned wilderness to begin with, the man who has tried to dehumanize every single person in this camp in one way or another?

It's as easy to pull the trigger in the direction of the running David Bruce as it was to punch him in the face this morning. Victor throws out his long arm like a piston, and the metal weight at the end of it cracks, sending a shudder through his whole body and a bullet flying across the river of insects that separates the two men. The first bullet disappears somewhere into the night. David Bruce, unharmed, begins to scream as he runs. Again the gun cracks in Victor's big hand. This time the bullet passes through David Bruce's back and out his chest. It flies on, to clang against the distant dozer David Bruce is breaking for. A skein of spraying blood mixes with the oily mist in the air from the diesel fire. With great gravity David Bruce spills forward. Tumbles. He slides amongst the bugs. He lies there, still alive. Screeching.

Victor thrusts his piston arm in a hard jolt for a third time and puts another bullet in him. This one seems to shear through David Bruce's body in some mysterious place, diverted by the world inside of him into a new, peculiar angle.

It kicks up dirt on the other side of his fallen body, making Victor imagine at first that he's missed him again. But the volume on David Bruce's retching turns down fast, and in seconds he is lying still and quiet.

Victor moves to tell Quent that it's over. They've finally stopped the killer among them. This nonsense is done. He turns to say this just in time to see the heavy pipe wrench Quent has been rattling around with since they left the dining area come crashing down on him. Beyond the incoming wrench, at arm's length, is Quent's screaming face as he delivers the frenzied blow.

VIII

Earlier in the night, Ian the mechanic lay inside the enveloped darkness of his makeshift bug net, a blanket tied by rope to a fabric loop in the tent ceiling and hung like an upside-down flower draped over his cot. Ian was fully clothed and sweat slicked from the stillness and heat of the enclosed space. He listened to the endless shifting shapes inside the insect song. He played over the many things he had seen since the song began breaking down the barricade between his dreams and the world. He listed all the curiosities he had managed to satisfy so far. But mostly his mind was engaged with the truck crash. He ran over it again and again.

He tried to cling to the little details of it. The bouncing roughness of the bug-glossed logging road, Samuel steering in hard jerks that only made small corrections as they rolled deeper into the woods, the truck's windshield wipers sweeping continuous cicadas from their field of vision, the rolled-up passenger window squirming with insects. It was as if the Chevy was crawling across the surface of another world. Ian remembered wanting to talk about it all. "These things, they've been beneath us this whole time. Living right under our feet. Waiting to eat and make more of themselves. It's a crazy business. Mystifying really. Beautiful in its way. Scary too . . . that this is how everything works."

Samuel, a more plain-spoken man, told Ian he'd never seen anything like it in all his life, and that was all he said on the matter. It was frustrating, the dearth of language, the silence where ideas could live. Not just from blunt Samuel, but from all the men, big and dumb and awkward and performing for one another. So Ian figured that was as good a time as any to take the long, yellow-handled Phillips screwdriver from his pocket and shove it into Samuel's throat as hard as he could.

The idea was to try to hit Samuel's Adam's apple with the point and see what kind of resistance Samuel's throat would give. How would Samuel respond? What would the action reveal? Would the blood come in a great spray, like from a hose under pressure? Or in a single, eruptive splatter that then sluggishly spurted in chunks, like the image Ian had in his mind when he heard the phrase "volcano of communism" on the radio?

Curiosity cried out for it. So Ian did the work. Samuel's Adam's apple was slippery under his skin and sectioned into separate parts of clustered cartilage. It cranked to the side of the onrushing, stabbing screwdriver. His neck popped, a little like a water balloon, but it did not spray. It spurted. This satisfied Ian's curiosity far more than pushing James into the cement mixer had, though that was not without its interesting outcome. Or poisoning Homer's coffee, which, frankly, had been a little boring.

Samuel, whose name is venerated in Christian, Jewish, and Muslim faiths, had kicked forward with his legs, landing heavy on both the gas and the clutch of the Chevy at the same time, causing the engine to rev. Samuel's hands sprung to the screwdriver sticking out of his throat. He gargled out a cry from some place deep in his animal mind, a wide-eyed shriek that struggled past the obstruction in his larynx.

The truck roared but didn't gain speed. Ian had to get his

own leg over and step on the gas pedal while shoving Samuel off the clutch. Samuel was gushing blood, slicking Ian as he struggled to get the Chevy into a wild lurch across the carpet of cicadas. The truck skidded off the logging road and slid in a sideways rush down an incline before coming to a hard stop on the driver's side against a prominent red maple. Ian's flat cap flew from his head, and the dead in the truck bed ejected into the woods from the impact.

It was thrilling to think about. Beating Fanny to death with a rock later that same night had satisfied many curiosities, and killing a woman had brought a new, different kind of elation. But that elation was nothing like the possibility of dying when Samuel's truck careened off the logging road, or the jarring confusion of the impact, or the vivid realization that he had actually survived once the crash was all said and done. The process of discovering that he was still breathing, glass riddled, heart racing, was easily the most exciting moment of his entire life.

He remembered the way he was pressed up against Samuel once the crash went quiet, almost in the man's arms, almost intimate. He remembered Samuel winding down, tiny convulsions and gurgling sounds coming from his body. Ian had pulled the screwdriver from Samuel's neck and its absence made a lazy faucet of clumpy blood surge in time with Samuel's slowing heart, spurting less with each beat. Samuel's eyes seemed dead before his body did, and if that were so, it was an unexpected mercy for good Samuel, Ian thought. He had always heard the brain died last.

Ian pulled himself out of the undamaged passenger side of the truck. He contemplated the pain in his neck, the bend in his back. Pain was an idea. Pain was interesting. Unable to walk at first, he sat on the ground. Once still, the cicadas surged up around him, crawling in his hair and over the gashes in his face. He tried to see how long he could go before he wiped them away. They crawled across his vision so that the sunlight came and went as their bodies blotted it out. The things that hide beneath our world, that wait, they are the weft of the weave, he thought. More a part of the pattern than that which we can see. After a time he had to blink tiny, clinging legs away from the surface of his eyes.

Gathered in his thoughts and finally calm in his heart, Ian had stood, achingly, his spine cinched pretty bad from the crash. He began to make his way back to the construction site, walking, wounded, through the insect calamity, thinking about how he would act when he told the others that Samuel was dead. Acting was an idea. Emotions were interesting.

Playing the event over and over again in his mind there on his cot, Ian the mechanic was lost in time, until his thoughts were interrupted by the sound of sliding sheets and the rustle of feet inside the tent. He peered out from his makeshift bug net. The first to slip out of the group sleeping area was sallow-eyed Baxter. But Baxter wasn't who Ian was the most curious about, not yet at least. The stimulation Baxter gave Ian had more to do with the way the young man was living through the events Ian had set into motion. Baxter's speculations and admissions at the sump fire, and how the others responded, had been deeply fascinating. No, Baxter was more interesting alive than dead, so Ian watched the boy move alone into the fire-haunted dark, but he did not follow.

Baxter wasn't sleepwalking, but he also didn't make a conscious choice to leave the tent. He didn't wonder if there was a killer on the loose or not. He didn't question his own safety as he left. He walked toward the signal fire. He didn't slow his approach as the heat increased. When he came to the fire's edge he did not stop to contemplate the severity of it. He kept walking. There was no hesitation before he stepped into the diesel pool with all the intention of a moth to a flame.

At first he dropped through the corona of heat on the surface of the pool and sunk fast into the oil beneath the fire.

But Baxter was taller than the sump's depth and once his feet settled against the concrete bottom his head lit like a struck match.

The sudden pain immediately wiped away Baxter's self, his id, the unconscious, any corner of his mind crafted from past experiences. Whatever was left of Baxter began to flail. His eyes boiled in his skull, his skin seared, his hair evaporated, his lungs inflated with black smoke, and his brain flash-dehydrated. Baxter managed to whip his arms over the threshold of the sump, where the base of the metal hatch would eventually go. There he became lifeless, propped, burning, creased in the middle over the concrete edge, half in and half out of the diesel pool. Cleansed and released by fire, as believers have been since the dawn of believing itself.

Ian was still awake some time later and was surprised when he heard another restless man in the tent. Again Ian peeked through the sliver of his hanging blanket. This time it was young Hank, wearing a heavy jacket despite the hot night. He too was leaving the safety of the tent. Hank suited Ian perfectly in that moment. A life's journey has a shape to it, an arc that lifts from childhood simplicity toward mounting bedlam, until we can no longer fathom the complexity of it and our little existence is finally made untenable. It was suddenly perfectly obvious that Hank was the next goal post in Ian's journey, in the shape of Ian's life. Circumstance created opportunity.

He followed Hank from afar, watching him enter the tarped-off dining area. After a moment of stillness and contemplation, Ian stepped in after him.

"Hank? I saw you leave the tent. I thought we were all going to stay together? Is everything okay?" Ian asked in the dark of the dining area.

It was a surprise when Hank pulled David Bruce's

handgun on him. Did Hank know that Ian had killed the others? Did it matter?

"What's that?" Ian asked.

"You fucking know what it is."

"Why'd you take it?"

"To keep me safe. To keep us safe from David Bruce. I got a real good look at Mrs. Stern. That wasn't no accident. You people can tell yourselves whatever gives you ease, but Victor and me, we saw that shit up close. So I took the gun. I took it."

"Okay. Honestly, I'd rather you have it than him. Maybe just don't point it at me though."

"But then I got to thinking." He tightened his sweaty hands on the grip. "If I went out by myself, maybe someone would follow me. Someone who wouldn't expect me to have this. The kind of man who could do another person harm, like they did Mrs. Stern. Then I could settle it, once and for all."

One thing Ian had learned throughout this whole experiment was that a man can know a thing. A man like Quent, say, can know that a man like Ian is a killer, as he clearly did yesterday when Ian came walking up to the clearing from the logging road covered in Samuel's blood. A man can know something like that in his soul, but then he'll let his mind talk his soul out of that knowing.

Ian wondered how far that truth could go. That was the new curiosity Hank held for Ian in the dark dining area, the gun between them. And so, as Hank was trying to say something—like, *So you tell me, why are you following me?* or *Stay right where the fuck you are!*—Ian was already crossing the space. Coming at Hank fast. How long would it take for the truth in Hank's soul to convince his mind that Ian was a man who wouldn't settle for anything less than one of them dying right there and right then? How long would Hank hesitate? How close could Ian get?

He came straight at Hank from door to dish area at gunpoint without Hank managing to pull the trigger. Ian thought Hank was the smartest of all the men he had hired (and didn't the surprise appearance of the gun prove that?). Maybe it was intellect that betrayed Hank, that kept him from committing to the gun, because it wasn't until Ian had his hands on the .45 that Hank finally pulled the trigger. By then Ian was able to use the energy of his forward momentum and the size of his own body, sleight as it was, to get up under the handgun, forcing a bend in Hank's elbows.

Ian didn't want the gun to go off; it wasn't ideal. There were still so many unanswered curiosities. But once the .45 was revealed, the odds of it staying silent were slim to none. By the time Hank, in a panic, told his finger to pull the trigger, his arms were bending into his chest and the gun was shoving itself forcefully up under his own chin.

Being so close to the gunshot, practically pressed face to face, was a religious experience for Ian. An angelic brightness engulfed both of them. When the brightness faded, Ian's ears were ringing and numb. Hank's chin had been re-sculpted, and the skull had misshapen in such a way that his suddenly bloodshot eyes stared off in different directions, farther apart than they'd been just a half-second before. Ian felt Hank's body lose all agency and surrender to the weight of itself, falling down like a tower in a controlled demolition. Hank's fragmented jaw caught Ian's vest as he slid from Ian's embrace, the vest that still had the blood of both the Sterns on it, popping buttons away like they were seeds being sown.

It was easily the most satisfying death so far, immediately replacing all the exhilarations of Samuel's murder. The confusion of the gun blast, Ian's proximity to his victim, the immediacy and spectacle of it all. And he was glad for it too, because that would have to be the last. The gunshot was fulfilling but unfortunate. The other men would be heading his way now.

Everyone would've heard it. They would make sure to come all together because a gunshot is a terrifying thing.

Ian had to admit to himself that it was over. He wouldn't have followed Hank if he knew Hank was the one who stole David Bruce's gun, but then wasn't that part of the journey too? The ultimate part? We ride our own actions until some surprise outcome throws us. We answer as many questions and curiosities as we can about the universe before the questioning gets the better of us. The trick was to enjoy the fall, and he certainly had.

Ian, the mechanic of all things, sat down with the gun in his hand. Is the end of the world coming? The communists? The bomb? A race war? A goddamned plague? Perhaps. Before, when he started to use his savings to pull all this together, it seemed inevitable that the world was ending. But now that his shelter would never be finished and he wouldn't be around to occupy it, he sort of hoped it wasn't the actual end of the world. It would be wasted on the others.

Ian put the barrel of the gun flush with his forehead. Just over the place where the ancient Asians believed the third eye resided. He remembered the last cicada emergence, which occurred when he was a boy. How many animals did he kill on those perfect summer days while the chorus rattled all around him? He'd been hearing that song in his head to varying degrees ever since. Never killing again, not even once, in all that time in between. Never harming a single person. Never raising his voice. Waiting. Turning into a man. Learning how to act around other people so that they could casually ignore him or at least not see the things that made him different. Plying a trade. Saving money. Keeping to himself. He began to plan for this last winter, knowing that it would be the summer of the emergence. He had waited until the very last moment to find stragglers who needed work and who no one would miss, plucking them from nomadic lives of obscurity, desperate to work no matter the job. Finding such men wasn't hard.

The cicadas came every summer, during a time of year the Romans called the dog days, but it wasn't the same. Not like this particular brood. The yearly cicadas often stopped their song at night. They came in much smaller numbers, and they were much less ambitious. No, this overwhelming commitment by nature that was happening all around them now was something that only occurred a few times in a man's life. All things considered, Ian found that he was happy he'd gotten as much done as he had. The men could've stopped him much sooner if they understood anything at all about nature and the way things truly worked. But the men understood nothing. They were drowning in their lack of understanding.

He thought so many things sitting there on the bench with the gun resting against his head. The day was over. His brain was filled with reasons and notions and curiosities both satisfied and unsatisfied. It was always too much chaos in there this time of day. Too confusing. First morning light meant clarity, but late nights meant chaos. The shape of a day is the same as the shape of a life. "Goodnight," he told himself. Maybe he sighed a little at the end, because the barrel angled slightly up as he pulled the trigger.

Ian was curious to understand what it felt like to be shot in the head. Dying is an idea. Dying is interesting. But he did not exist long enough to resolve his curiosity. The force of the gun propelled his lifeless hand away from his face and the .45 flew across the dining area.

IX

IX

THE GUN FLIES from Victor's hand as Quent's wrench knocks Victor's left shoulder out of its socket. Victor shambles backward and lets out a howl of pain. Quent remembered Hank saying Victor had a southpaw stance in his boxing days, so Quent has circled to Victor's left, taking out the lethal arm first. But more strategy than that is too much chess for a man like Quent, and now it's a free-for-all as he brings the wrench down again. Victor protects his head with his right arm and the wrench lands hard against his forearm so that his whole frame shudders from the hit.

Victor is out of Quent's range on the third drop of the wrench and moving back faster than his big body would suggest possible. Quent knows he can't let the maniac gather himself. Victor is a man of violence, Quent thinks. A man who has been treated like shit his whole life because of the color of his skin. A man who was turned evil by other men's hate. For the first time it occurs to Quent that maybe someone had hurt his own father when he was young too, just as his father had hurt Quent, as Quent has hurt others.

The wrench swings wide and wild. It carries Quent's weight forward more than he means it to. Victor has time to gather himself. In everything Victor does he is faster than Quent. He nails Quent hard with a right jab that whips Quent's head back and forth as if his neck is a spring. But Quent is rabid. He swings the wrench with abandon. When the wrench hits, the wrench hurts. Quent is driving Victor backward alongside the sump fire. The air is boiling and oily.

Victor manages to get his hands on Quent's wrench. He yanks Quent around by the tool, pulling him off his feet. But Quent doesn't let go. Quent screams. Victor's left shoulder is destroyed. As he yanks on the wrench, the pain strikes through him like lightning. One last big heave and Quent goes into the fire.

But Quent is thrown so hard by Victor that he clears the burning sump, flying over Baxter's blackened corpse. Parts of his canvas trousers catch fire around his shins and he ends up tumbling hard down the concrete stairs and into the bomb shelter.

At the bottom of the shelter, he thrashes at his trousers. He feels the heat on his skin before he manages to put it out. Stabs of pain ring up his legs where his hands fall in his effort to smother the flames. Some of his ribs feel broken from the fall, and his face is scraped badly from the concrete. There's blood streaming from his nose in an endless spill from Victor's jab. He needs to get to his feet, he needs to keep moving, but everything hurts so much.

There are climbing holds in the back wall of the shelter where the emergency rear hatch was eventually to be set. Quent knows that's his only way out of this dark, concrete pit. Narrow ditches set for the air, electrical, and plumbing are obstacles in the blackness and everything is slick with leaping cicadas. Above him the roof is just a lattice rebar grid with wooden beams set into a partially constructed form with temporary props holding it up. Since the beams were never poured, the roof form was never completed.

For a moment Quent doesn't know where Victor is. He

achingly, cautiously, starts to head toward the back of the shelter, using one of the thick walls to support himself, but then he hears Victor's voice come down from the edge of the hole that the shelter has been set into. Victor is yelling down at him over the insect chorus and the fire's roar.

"Quent! Listen to me! I don't believe you're the killer! I don't see it in you. And I know . . . I know I ain't the killer! So we can be done, right now. You hearing me down there?"

Quent peers up through the lattice roof form. He's not sure if he can see Victor moving above. He's starting to think that maybe he burned his feet and shins real bad because his trouser legs have grafted to his skin in a blackened weave. His shoulders start to shake with sadness, and when he tries to talk his voice sounds like a wail. "No! No . . . the killer wasn't David Bruce. No . . . when you . . . when you shot Ian and Hank, David was with me! He was on his cot! No, Victor! It can only be you! It can only be you!" And then there are no more words, just the warble of Quent trying to contain his own pain.

Victor's voice comes again from the sky, the horrible sky, from where God metes out suffering. "Does anybody even know you're out here, Quent?"

Quent understands what Victor's really asking.

"Naw . . . nobody. You?"

"No. I don't think none of us had anyone who knew where we were."

If there were a deeper pit of despair for Victor to sink into, he's never known it. There's only one way out of this for him. Quent can't live. He's the last white man here and he doesn't believe Victor is innocent. Quent won't stand up for him when the outside world arrives and starts making conclusions. Victor needs to silence Quent and then get as far away from this place as he can as soon as he can.

It's hard for him to see Quent down in the darkness of the

shelter through the half-constructed roof form. Victor stalks the edge of the backfill ditch that surrounds the sunken outer concrete walls, casting about for him. Sometimes he thinks he sees movement, but he can never be sure. He could go down there and confront him or wait for Quent to pull himself up the back. But Victor doesn't want to look a man in the face when he kills him, so he pulls the trigger at the first hint of motion below. The bullet pings off of rebar and shatters wood, sending it away from Quent, who screams out at the sound of the gunshot.

"Jesus! Fuck! Why, Victor? Why? Why kill us all? Why did we have to die out here?"

Victor fires again. Again the webbing of the roof form between Victor and Quent causes him to miss. He's firing with his non-dominant right hand because his left arm is useless, and the rock of the gun rolls through his shoulders, causing Victor to yelp out in pain each time he shoots.

After the second shot Victor can hear Quent sobbing down in the dark. "Do you really hate us so much?" Quent yells up at him. Victor pulls the trigger again, girding himself against the pain. He's got to get this done if he hopes to survive. He's got to shut the pitiful, sobbing man up. But the hammer drops dry. That's all the killing the gun has in it for the night. Somehow Quent knows the .45 is done because Victor can hear him call out, "Oh, thank God! Thank God!"

Now Victor can see Quent climbing up out the back of the shelter where the rear hatch would be. Quent drags himself out of the hole and awkwardly, barely, leaps across the backfill ditch with tremendous effort. Then he limps furiously for the tree line, weeping as he stumbles toward the wilderness.

Victor plunges into the woods after him. The night is dark. The woods are thick. It's as if they're swimming through cicadas. Existence becomes impressionistic. Both men suffer. Victor's pain is in his shoulders and arms, but Quent's pain is in his ribs, his feet, and his legs, so Victor is gaining on him fast. Both men ache profoundly in their hearts. Quent trips.

Suddenly there is a man straddling him, wrapping his hands around Quent's neck. Quent is a little boy in his bed. Quent is screeching and screeching and kicking and kicking against the big man in his bed, fighting him in a way he never did before, in a way he always wished he had. The chorus rises. Through the trees he can see the distant signal fire that was meant to save them.

His throat collapses under the crushing force of the big hands. Quent opens his mouth as wide as he can in a desperate gasp for air. The cicadas pile in. They've wanted to get inside of him from the very beginning. The whole brood has labored for this moment, this gaping mouth.

Two men. Victor closes his eyes so he doesn't have to see the insects swarm Quent's swollen face and fill his open mouth as he chokes him. Victor's hands ratchet tighter and tighter. Quent kicks and convulses. It takes a long time. It takes years and years. It takes all of time. Then there is only one man. Finally. Victor begins to cry.

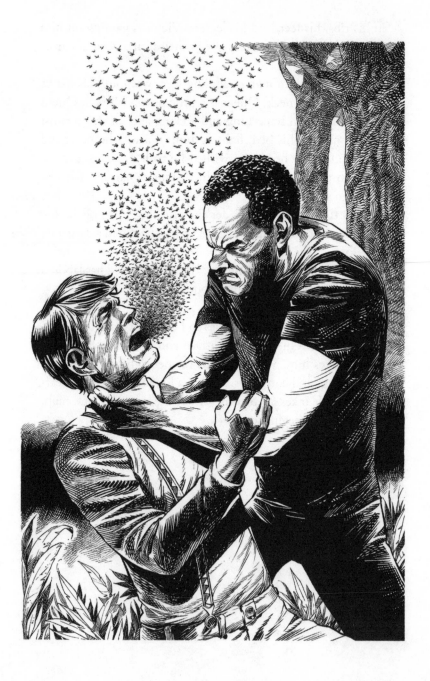

VICTOR HAS TO KEEP MOVING. He's lost all sense of direction in the dark, but at some point he'll find a road. He must. If he can just keep from being discovered in the vicinity of the construction site when someone responds to the signal fire, if he can just slide back into civilization somehow, then he'll get out of this. Not okay, not unscathed, but free. They'll go looking for a killer, of course, they'll forever be looking for a killer, but they won't come looking for him.

The song is so loud out here in the utter wilderness. Victor flogs at himself to keep the cicadas off of his exposed skin. His eyes flare wildly in the hopes that he'll see better in the darkness if he widens them as much as possible, his whole face flexing with the effort. He has visions, hallucinations, sees phantoms, and hears voices in the insect chorus. Quent's voice, gasping, choking, dying.

He suddenly remembers what he was trying to tell Quent when the two men were looking over dead Samuel inside the wrecked truck. There was no tree branch. Ian had said a tree branch busted into the cab and killed Samuel, but Victor wanted to point out that it wasn't there. Yet the song was so clamorous, like it is now, that Victor had lost his will to think. This is just a musing among a squall of memories and emotions and illusions, rising and falling, each fleeting. None of it is real, survival is the only thing that's ever been real, and he's still got sense enough to know that.

END

ACKNOWLEDGMENTS

Thanks to Tze Chun and Sebastian Girner at TKO who, for reasons completely unknown to me, seemed to inherently believe I could pull off prose and who have shepherded this work from pasture to pen with incredible story insight. It has changed shape more than once, and they never even batted an eye.

And to Amy Sumerton. She came onboard at the eleventh hour and, with minimum fuss and maximum fun, made it all so much better. She's the copy-editor I've always dreamed of having.

Many other friends and loved ones have put eyes on this and helped me sharpen it:

Kelly Bruce has read every single draft with enthusiasm. Believing in me more than I believe in myself.

Luis Reyes read the first draft with the original structure and then sat down with me in a Long Beach dive bar, back when the world was still turning, to give me his thoughts. His creative zeal has been a signal fire for me for over seventeen years now.

Tony Davies combed over it with the eyes of a true builder, authenticating and improving the construction sequences I had cobbled together from my half-remembered days as a young man in the labor trenches.

And Arvid Nelson, who I've had the pleasure of knowing for two decades now, gave a read to the first draft that sported the final structure. His side-eyeing of my word usage and theme implementation was invaluable.

No one achieves anything alone.

Thank you all.

—Joshua

ABOUT THE AUTHOR

JOSHUA DYSART is a multiple Eisner-nominated writer of books such as *Hellboy, Swamp Thing, Conan, Harbinger, Bloodshot, BPRD,* and *Violent Messiahs.* He wrote the critically-acclaimed *Unknown Soldier* for Vertigo, as well as a graphic novel based on Neil Young's album *Greendale.* It spent two weeks at #3 on the *New York Times* bestseller list. In 2017, Dysart received the Dick Giordano Humanitarian Award for his work bringing stories from destabilized regions of the world to comic books.

ABOUT THE ILLUSTRATOR

Born in 1972, M.K. PERKER started his professional career at the age of seventeen. He worked for all major newspapers of his native Turkey along with the Turkish editions of *Esquire, Cosmopolitan, FHM, Harper's Bazaar, InStyle,* and *Madame Figaro* before moving to the States in 2001. His illustration, comics, and cartoons have been published in the *New York Times, New Yorker, Mad Magazine, Washington Post, Wall Street Journal, Heavy Metal, The Progressive,* and *Columbia Journalism Review.* He co-created and illustrated the graphic novel *Cairo* and the Eisner-nominated monthly series *Air* with writer G. Willow Wilson for DC/Vertigo. He wrote and illustrated the graphic novel *Insomnia Cafe* for Dark Horse Comics. He co-created and illustrated the mini-series *Todd the Ugliest Kid on Earth* with writer Ken Kristensen for Image Comics. He also illustrated several issues of *The Unwritten, Fables, and The Dreaming* for DC/Vertigo. His comics have appeared in several anthologies, such as *The Escapist, The Noir* for Dark Horse and *Time Warp* for DC/Vertigo. He has illustrated more than ten novels and created hundreds of book covers for Turkish publishers.

Get behind-the-scenes content,

including early drafts, notes,

and inspirations from the

writer and illustrator.

TKOPRESENTS.COM
/BROODX-BONUS

PICK UP THE OTHER TITLES IN OUR FIRST WAVE OF ILLUSTRATED NOVELLAS!

One Eye Open

By Alex Grecian
Illustrated by Andrea Mutti

After her mother's sudden passing, Laura and her daughter Juniper return to her childhood home in the rural outskirts of Denmark. In the scenic village amidst seas of wheat fields, Laura hopes they have finally left tragedy behind them. Juniper begins to notice something strange about the people she encounters. In tracing her lineage back, Juniper makes a horrifying discovery. This town is alive with more than just nature, and the endless fields of wheat demand to be harvested, whether the hands that do so are alive or dead . . .

An occult thriller about coming home and the monsters that await us there. By *New York Times* bestselling author Alex Grecian (*The Yard*) with illustrations by Andrea Mutti.

$9.99

Blood Like Garnets

By Leigh Harlen
Illustrated by Maria Nguyen

A modern-day witch can knit the dead back to life for a fearsome price. Follow a lone predator's surprising night on a bloody hunt. Join a carefree karaoke night with friends that ends in blood, tears, and dark revelations.

Beneath the placid surface of family, love, and reason, the line between monster and human blurs, love becomes obsession, and voices long silenced demand to be heard in Leigh Harlen's blood-curdling debut.

Dive into the terrors that lurk behind every corner and in every shadow with these flesh-crawling tales. Contains eight spine-tingling horror stories by Leigh Harlen with illustrations by Maria Nguyen.

$9.99

TKO
PRESENTS